TRYATHON

THE LOVE OF A GALAXY

RALPH SMART

INFINITE WATERS PUBLISHING INC.

COPYRIGHT

Book Cover Illustrations by INFINITE WATERS & SARAH HOLMLUND

Graphic Design by INFINITE WATERS

Published by INFINITE WATERS Publishing Inc.

International Standard Book Number (ISBN): 978-0-9568973-1-2

Printed in the United Kingdom

CONTENTS

FOREWORD

NEW LONDON 2049 AD

WE LIVED IN THE DIGITAL AGE, FUTURE WARS WOULD BE FOUGHT THROUGH TECHNOLOGY.

New London's architecture kept growing: they built buildings out of nothing. Foreign entities created illusions through architecture, vast labyrinths—worlds within worlds. Distinguishing authentic worlds from fake ones became challenging, even for the greatest of minds. Cast under a spell, tricked. Foreign entities understood numbers, they took advantage of them. They acquired power, dominion over all kingdoms on—'Earth.'

"I hear the screams from Earth: screams of a billion prisoners: screams of abandoned children from their mothers: what have we become?"

"We have seen Earth disintegrate into a handful of ash. We watch your master manipulators create famines, debt—prisons to house you in. How they create endless languages to keep you divided. We watch the 'Undesirables' perpetuate false claims: a myriad of lies. A world full of screens, lots of squares, no circles. Tryathon has seen it all, and we will watch no—further.

"IN THE AGE OF TECHNOLOGY, EARTH IS STARVED OF WISDOM." – HATHORA

ACKNOWLEDGEMENTS

This book is dedicated to anyone who dreams of a better world. Praises pour out to my marvellous mother for being a huge inspiration, and to my wonderful sister for always being there—I love you both. A big thanks to the universal creator—birthing all.

Much gratitude to the whole Infinite Waters radio family.

I feel blessed to have connected with so many beautiful minds through my travels, and all the marvellous people I continue to meet. I thank everybody who made it possible for me to write this book.

Some people may classify this novel as a science fiction thriller: I classify it as a novel which seeks to challenge us all, how we see the world around us: a novel which seeks to question the nature of reality.

Sharing these writings, I feel honoured. The book was so much fun to write—allowing me to explore what we all have—our imagination.

Imagination is a marvellous gift—when you open it.

I hope this book will inspire people to realise, they are the power they seek. Let no one tell you that you cannot do something. Many people will try to prevent you from doing something, because they do not know what to do themselves.

I thank the universes, the galaxies, and all the stars shining for us.

A special shout out to all the artists out there. Civilisations were created from the minds of artists: it is the artist, which creates—worlds.

Stay creating—fulfil the dream.

MUCH LOVE

INFINITE WATERS

CHARACTERS OF TRYATHON

Sylvannus—Writer, dreamer, alchemist, architect, number maker

Luz—Visionary, clairvoyant, architect, number maker

Pandora—Word architect, natural healer, number maker

Proteus—Freedom fighter, hacker, architect, number maker

Gothlin—Number maker, adept, truth seeker

Dr. Sebastian Jacques Pingo—Head researcher of 'Everest'

Tronan—'New London's' city dictator

Nephli—Wife of Tronan, seer, clairvoyant

Hathora—Oracle of Tryathon

Streams of Light—inhabitants of Tryathon

Memners—The Crystals

Governor of Neptis—Ruler of Planet: 'Neptis'

The Circle of Trust—The Hidden Order

Rosney—Tronan's closest associate

The X-matron—The future car of 2049 AD: Wired to emotions, self-recharging whilst driving: An intelligent design. The black machine: Underwater capabilities: Hover car: Aerodynamic: Self-automated: Remote controlled: Changing paint colours: Holographic windows: Laser proof: Spy cameras: Inbuilt surveillance

Lasers—Silent weapons of warfare

Blue Trains—Laser speed trains running throughout 'New London' city.

PROLOGUE

2049 JANUARY 1ST CANARY WHARF 'NEW LONDON'

Gothlin—"What if I told you something you were not ready to hear? Would you still listen?

It seems to be the only way, the last resort. In time, all will be revealed, this is what I do know.

When you least expect—surprise! It always happens."

Sylvannus—"I am not sure if I am ready for this: I am not sure my mind is—clear enough."

Gothlin—"It all begins with the first step, even before you can walk."

Sylvannus—"I know, I know."

Gothlin—"So, what's this talk of Tryathon?"

Sylvannus—"Well, it's the land of many things we want—freedom."

Gothlin—"And how far away is it?"

Sylvannus—"That we cannot measure (laughing), nearer than farther."

Gothlin—"And how do you hope to get there?"

Sylvannus—"I was hoping you could help us with that."

Gothlin—"I see."

HUMANITY'S FIRE

SYLVANNUS'S JOURNAL 2049, JUNE 10TH

When I started life, my aim was to conquer the world in its entirety—to own it.

Now, as I journey through this barren land, I strive not to become consumed by it.

I have seen humanity's fire, after all I was the one who helped set it alight.

However, the fire has raged for too long—unhealthy.

I watch as it continues to burn everything in its path, like a stubborn child, refusing to look when crossing the road.

It's heat has caused many to perish prematurely, its wrath, unyielding—merciless.

The wise say:

"When a fire has consumed everything, the only thing left for the fire to consume is itself."

But how much longer must this fire go on?

"How much longer must we burn with it?"

CHAPTER ONE

SEPTEMBER 5TH (2049 AD)

"WHAT'S THE WORLD BECOMING?"

THE waters glistened, crystals sapphire blue: we stared, with thoughts of becoming them. We lived in an open space by the sea, on 'The Outskirts.' Earth had changed in the last three thousand years, but more in the last twenty. The four of us lived in 'Praa Sands, South West Cornwall': golden sand beaches: 'Could you blame us?' 'New London' was dead, a soulless city with no heart, run by machines. Two years gone already: seems like yesterday. We still visited our families in the city—what was left of it.

Society's fabric had changed entirely. Computers became extensions of us. The machines made themselves more than comfortable: your reality, but not ours. Fleeing the city was part of our destiny: nature ushered us to. We saw the signs: what this city was becoming. Children were no longer in schools, there were none. Obsolete since 2045: they no longer served their purpose. The world slept in our palms: holographic computers allowed children to home study: an interaction of mutual exchange. Hearts raced pumping out streams of data—flooding us.

'What were we becoming? What would be our fate?'

Once again we found ourselves stuck at the crossroads: humanity's divide. Information saturated us, we swam in it: storing more than we could download. Screens disappeared: we became the monitors. Nobody in the city cared for privacy anymore: we gave up our rights a long time ago.

Libraries closed, banks shut, and the city smelled like eviscerated dog carcasses. Ashen grey clouds swarmed inbetween roads to provoke us. The masses' intestines churned out sick from uproars, our disease—ignorance. Angry protest banners read: "NEW INFRASTRUCTURE: SERVICES WHICH SERVE US MORE EFFICIENTLY." Disgruntled protestors lingered on overcrowded pavements 'til dark, their nostrils flaring with rage. Tumultuous gasps reverberated off concrete buildings, the city's anthem. Beads of sweat formed on brows, faces emaciated from sheer exhaustion.

Hospitals closed on rates of once a week. Due to financial restraints, many doctors and nurses became redundant. There was no space: we lived suffocating: the city exceeded its threshold. Rose blood boiled, bursting city veins: London became—unrecognisable. People traded whatever they could get their hardened hands on. Paper money became old fashioned: it carried babyish weight. Eyes were credit cards: we identified ourselves through '*biometric authentication.*' Irises stored passwords for years of life—savings.

The increasing city's population became overwhelming: hence we fled elsewhere. Society's last breath was being breathed—there was no respirator. Blood stains cardinal red, graffitied city walls, smudging signatures everywhere. Chunks of ice could be felt in the depths of the city's throat, cutting us like daggers. Corporations located in the city were becoming extinct. Every parasite needed a host and nobody was willing to host them.

'How vast was 'Earth'? What were 'Earth's' true origins? Why did the truth always seem to be shrouded in mysterious covers?'

Darkened newspapers buried in godforsaken alleys wafted with winds which trawled abreast. "The papers" were seen as fossils, on par with dinosaurs. Publishers were not printing: their ink had run dry. Fortunately or unfortunately, everything must change: the great paradox of life. Upgrades in multifarious assortments were sewn into humanities cloth. 'Blotix,' called "The Universal Mind" by experts: epitomised the future: 2049. Mammoth in design: a digital bottomless pit: heralded by scientists globally as—'The New Messiah.' A world within a world: once entering Blotix, you were sure to be lost—forever.

Police dwindled in numbers throughout the city, helped by a few volunteers dressed in liquorice black leather jackets. Scattered groups felt God ordained them: anointing their heads with jasmine oils to uphold law and order. Referring to themselves as *'The Protectors'*: their fingers plagued with thick yellow calluses, illustrated grim scars of war. City crime rates soared. Charcoal black rats crawled around neglected street lampposts, like wild dogs unshackled from leashes. The city was a desolate war zone, living out its—nightmares.

'Who was in charge of 'New London'? Where were its leaders?'

Politicians were nowhere to be seen: the city became rudderless. Heaps piled to discuss the future. People took laws into their own hands, affirming it a part of destiny. Beryl red bloodshot eyes shone during the day, illuminating into the darkest nights. Magnolia white cigarette smoke impregnated the naked air. Asphalt tar stuck to lungs lined with mucous filth: coughing—the only way to breathe. Gangrene fingernails flaked upon tired streets. Stubborn addicts twirled in drunken states, as they continued dancing with devils.

Life threatening viruses seldom oozed into *Blotix's* pores, infiltrating them. The immune system had been compromised once before: but not to this treacherous capacity. Treated as a high threat of maximum security, a nuisance: bloody catastrophe. Hidden truths lay bare flesh: vulnerable, scabby. Revealing clues, answers to the ultimate riddle:

"What is this place called 'Earth'?"

Challenging our perceptions, stretching minds: transporting us to the extraordinary. Earth's appearance deceived the best of us: deciphering brought us closer to the ultimate—truth.

Copious amounts of mischief spawned after the advent of the venomous virus's conception. Nobody sprang forth: its troublesome culprit remained notoriously anonymous. Disrupted holographic computers temporarily froze like Siberian glaciers—frosted blades.

Rumours surfaced:

"Was it premeditated? It's inconceivable."

Disturbing lunch, the poisonous virus materialised in the form of a thirty minute public service announcement. Agitated shoulders shrugged, while hot food became cold. Caught laughing in stitches, taking it for a hoax: a satirical affair. Nothing surprised anybody anymore: the world in 2049 AD had seen it all. I peer at society as it cremates itself alive, as the world becomes—blinder.

Nothing was open, airports throughout England were closed. Giant weights thrashed against bare bones: we sought its antithesis. Stagnant waters filled disregarded pot holed roads. Foul sewer stench from mucky putrid undigested meat could be smelt in our sleep—we deserved more. Superfluous lifestyles: society became a bunch of spoilt children.

"How did we find each other?"

Birds of the same feather flock together: like attracts like. Luz, Proteus, Pandora, and I were as close knit as a raspberry *'Bellini'* garment, freshly shelved. We shared similar world views, attitudes, demeanours, and sensibilities. Free spirits was our excuse for leaving 'New London' and slipping off into the plush watermelon gold 'Outskirts, Praa Sands'.

'Praa Sands' was a renowned surfing paradise facing the 'Atlantic Ocean': pronounced locally as 'Pray Sands': a mile long idyllic white sandy beach to roam wild. Lying south of the *A394 Helston to Penzance* road— an unspoilt pearl: Cornwall's best kept secret. Five hours driving from 'New London' diminished our animated eyes into refrigerated corpses. Anaesthetised torsos, debilitated vertebras: slithering like slugs endeavouring to break their fragile calcium carbonate shells. Squinting out of flat glass windows into emerald blue waters: marvelling at the pristine coastline's lustrous grandeur. Unconstrained salt water aromas nonchalantly seeped into our bare barren nostrils: we had—arrived.

Whooshing sounds of waves crashed, intermingling with voices of Peregrine Falcons hollering each other, circling aimlessly into the Moroccan velvet skyline. The horizon caught glimpses of us, as twirling waters swayed to contact each other. Waters stretched farther than our eyes could distinguish. Buoyant man eating *'Mako'* sharks patrolled recklessly underneath, safeguarding occult treasures. Lemon blossom lights penetrated the ocean's expanse, snoozing on its surface. Breaking ripples flowed towards us, forming thick frothy coconut cream white foam. Glaring at lush ambrosial greenery: surrounded by ancient medieval castle cliffs. Overwhelming enchantment left us close-mouthed and speechless—searching for words.

EARTHSHIPS

'Earthships' were sustainable eco-friendly buildings generally built from earth filled tires, or other recyclable materials. Earth's natural resources were harnessed to garner energy. Thermally insulated with adobe: an organic material comprised of sand, clay, and water. Adobe structures were immensely durable, accounting for some of the oldest prevailing buildings in the world. Ample volumes of thermal energy kept the house cool in summer and baking in winter: the best of both worlds. Fibreglass cisterns harvested rainwater cascading from the roof through two spiralling vortex filters. Building upon a vacated caravan camp site, we worked our tortured fingers to the brink of death. Pandora was the architect: her imagination lasted centuries.

Luz cherished the garden: being in nature's womb freed her. Gliding splendour fingers through rough grass: her deep brown walnut eyes stared in admiration at life's miracles. Vegetables planted from neighbouring land plots reminded us food was not scarce. Once again, soaking rain seduced the soil: we lived in abundance. Mini groups kindred to ours lived close by: feelings of mutual appreciation were shared.

"Why did they come here? Why did we?" everyone had their reason.

The digital age prompted many to leave the city, to reconnect with nature. Mucus thick technology saturated Earth's coagulated plague ridden arteries: blocking them. The so called famine ridden *"Third world countries,"* all disappeared. Africa possessed more machines than anywhere else: becoming a base hoarding them. Automated drones with abilities to set up camps where they chose—roamed lands—they governed them.

Nanotechnology made it possible to build machines at subatomic levels. Manufacturing abundant resources allowed us control over biochemical processes in our bodies, enabling us to eliminate disease and unwanted aging. *'Nanobots,'*: robots as miniscule as viruses, injected pomegranate red bloodstreams. Programmed to reproduce themselves— the new cure for cancer. Society's main religion became *'Transhumanism.'* A way of life suggesting humanity should aspire to higher levels, physically, mentally and socially. Technology's accelerating velocity swerved clumsily: crashing throughout the city like wild *'Indianola Texas'* hurricanes.

Human enhancements were widely available for sale. They sold smiles lasting forever—irreplaceable.

Ancient forgotten scrolls predicted the coming change: foreseeing humans would become remnants, memories—ancient souvenirs. *'Mind transfer'* was a process of mapping biological brain blueprints and copying them into a holographic computer. Uploading human consciousness onto computers became tradition: celebrated like—independence festivals.

Many groups were defiant. Scattered resistances charged into 'Trafalgar Square', unruly: fully opposing human enhancements.

"We're killing ourselves, losing touch with ourselves and nature: what's a life worth?" Seas of howls were heard like shattered glass screams.

'FIFTY YEARS IS ALL WE HAVE LEFT,' infuriated banners read, whilst hisses of saliva exchanged between street police and angry protestors.

Genetically engineered chestnut dark *'Presa Canario'* dogs attempted to free themselves from tight leashes as copious artificial liquids dripped onto grounds beneath. Their mouths became slobbering oceans. Towering ten feet in height – they became the city's protection. Powerful constructions: harsh textured flat coats, cuboid boxed heads, robust steroid inoculated cylindrical muscular necks. Undercover police stationed behind *'Nelson's column,'* steered remote controllers. Vicious snarls from tweaked commandment settings, delivering extra volatile performances. Technology became the new weapon of warfare.

The city never slept. Brain-computer interfaces promised amplified intelligence. City dwellers branched into two bands: some for the latest scientific interventions, others firmly against it. Gates had opened which were once closed, however, making lives effortless was questionable: science often flung out claims which were phoney.

Scientists predicted *'Z Voice Modifiers'* would change the human voice forever. A substantial majority throughout the city purchased the swanky *'Z Voice Modifiers'*: feeling *'chic'*—boastful about their investment. Emerging modern technology allowed users opportunities to modulate voice tone intonations without a hitch. Authentic voices—fought to be heard.

Our voices travelled across the ocean. 'Praa Sands's,' coast offered excellent exit routes. Wide arrays of possibilities gaped at us in a manifold of directions. If need be, we would swim: develop hypothermia: whatever it took for our—freedom.

'Being Free Is Your Birthright,' hung low in a silver plated rosewood frame in the corner of our living room. 'Praa Sands' was a world away from London, Hampstead, where I grew up. London was a crazy city: however, it was full of interesting—people.

I met Proteus *'The Wizard'* in *'Hampstead Heath,' North West London.* Exquisitely rich in history, fauna, flora and heritage. The *'Heath'* embraced over eight hundred magical glades, woodland, heathland, and meadows. Six hundred and fifty different species of flowering plants and ferns dwelt there. *'Kingfishers,' 'Reed Warbles,'* and *'British Woodpeckers'*—chilled in exuberant habitats. Ancient *'Beech Trees'* paused still, while *'Noctule Bats,'* Britain's largest, rose before sunset from their roosts. Summer fever encouraged people to lunge themselves head first: diving into ice cool refreshing *'Baths.'*

Proteus wore huckleberry blue corduroy trousers with ripped seams kissing the grass. Friday was *'strolling day'* for me. *'Hampstead Heath,'* helped alleviate my wrecked mind. Molten wax dripped cunningly on my forehead, leaving vile indents. Jammed solid and tight in between the cities wicked crutches: an abused cranium rattled inside. Exasperated by life's stresses: searching for answers. Ill-at-ease facial muscles twitched, bulging out involuntarily: I became vermin. Dashing to and fro, immersed inside gluey endless webs. *'Status anxiety'* pervaded my aura, society's cough—contagious.

"Why do so many of us wear masks during the day, and take them off at night?"

Costume changes were becoming too tedious for my liking: total nonsense. Handing out *'curriculum vitae's'*: aspiring to acquire approvals, from employers I never knew—total strangers. Those were the days of hovering in the dry wilderness: floating in limbo, similar to lose leaves, disconnected from—withering branches.

Unfurling his *'Daddy longlegs'* buffed fingernails, Proteus spread them across his glossy rosewood, *'Admira Solista'* guitar. Delicate fingers picked transparent nylon strings. Playing the immortal *'Tom Jobim's'* classic, *'Garota de Ipanema'* (Girl from Ipanema)—my favourite. We spoke together on the power of music:

"Music is a universal language, conveying messages from distant worlds" he said warmly.

It appears being born in the sand, sun, and sea simultaneously was a divine blessing. *'Bossa Nova'* oozed through my capillaries:

'What more can I say?'

Proteus was not as inspired as I, with respect to *'Bossa Nova'*; although his best friend adored it—Luz. Personifying beauty, she displayed a unique freshness. The three of us met every Sunday in *'Hampstead Heath,'* discussing worldly affairs—*'the digital age.'* After several months transpired, Pandora, an old childhood friend of mine accompanied us. Four kindred spirits in *'the garden,'* supported by each other's strength. Pandora and I shared similar plights; both stuck in dead end jobs; two limping city rats, hobbling to finish—the race.

Luz never took life so serious, making me attracted to her laid back approach. Her honey comb fragrance was enough incentive alone for our fortnightly meetings. She possessed a magnetic charm—a fatal attraction. Enjoying Pandora's company, feeling all women should—maintain their bond. Pandora was a *'twin soul Gemini'*; at certain moments infatuated with life; at others, not. Three years of developing impermeable foundations, made us see each other's—true worth.

'Praa Sands' arose, when Luz said:

"Why don't we live by the sea?"

Ruminating on her words, she had sown seeds within us; invigorating ideas which swam like whirlwinds in our minds. Travelling became more alluring—than ever.

Light summer breezes tapped shoulders, as we made the necessary arrangements to travel. The *'rat race'* would be no longer.

Waving *'good-byes'* to our families; telling them we would return, but we couldn't—'Praa Sands' became home.

Removing ourselves from the city, placed life in guillotine sharp perspectives: we knew—naught. Life in the city was a trivial pursuit: keeping us mindlessly distracted to what was really happening on Earth.

Seven new planets had been found since 2033 AD. 'Tryathon,' a favoured topic in our conversations, kept us entertained. We remembered being distant star travellers: the only question entering our minds:

"HOW THE HELL DO WE GET THERE?"

THE CROSSROADS

SYLVANNUS'S JOURNAL 2049, FEBRUARY 9TH

Are you pro–life or pro–death?

Do you live to nurture or do you live to destroy?

Do you live to sustain or do you live to waste?

Do you live to compete or do you live to work together?

Who is my enemy?

Who has become the villain of my story?

Who have I let into my house?

There must come a time when you see the stop sign.

When you realise you have exceeded limits.

What drives you?

Have you not seen the damage inflicted upon yourself?

Your lifestyle has become cancerous.

Where will you go? Where can you go?

You have killed everything: your addiction has become your madness—a terrible disease.

You live through the persona, your mask.

I have never ever seen the real you:

"Who are you?"

CHAPTER TWO

"WHAT'S IN A NUMBER?"

FROM the beginning of time, few have wandered 'Earth,' possessing extraordinary talents: endowed with sublime gifts beyond measure. Throughout the ages they were described as, *'otherworldly,'* becoming highly sought after. Delicately detailed, carved engravings adorned ancient temple wall linings, offering homage. These unique beings were widely acclaimed, idolised, *'immortalised.'* From: ancient *'Thebes'* (Greece), *'Elam'* (Iran), *'Sumer'* (Iraq), *'Kemet'* (Egypt), *'Etrusca'* (Asia Minor), *'Maya'* (Peru), *'Tenochtitlán'* (Mexico), *'Angkor Wat'* (Cambodia), *'Ionia'* (Turkey), *'Khajuraho'* (India), to *'Pompeii'* (Rome): they were deified—*'Gods.'*

Such magical beings could mutate their bodies. Harness *'Chi'* (breath): channelling it throughout their bodies—transforming raw air into gold—harmonising souls. Empowered by *'Telekinesis,'* possessing abilities to manipulate *'matter'* with their minds. Bestowed powers of *'augmentation'* granted them permission to alter others' *'life force energy'* at will. Possessing: accelerated healing processes, under water breathing, X-ray vision, supernatural durability, telescopic/microscopic sight: they were—*'versatile creatures.'*

The *elixir* of life is water. Waves sway in the ocean, through *'Breaths'*: inhaling and exhaling. Few of Earth's inhabitants mastered the science of *'breath'*: expelling *'airs'* on par with agitated *'West palm beach'* twisters. Inhalations levelled powers of fierce *'gravitational vortexes'*. Other gifts included super swift reflexes, and maintained lightning speed actions and reactions—before thoughts. There were those walking amongst us who lived—forever.

Small minorities, exhibiting *'invulnerability,'* possessed immunities from every kind of Earthly harm. Hercules, son of 'God'—*Zeus*, *Artemis* 'Goddess' of the wilderness, daughter of 'Goddess'—*Leto*:

Sekhmet 'Goddess' of war, daughter of 'God'–'*Ra*', *Anubis* 'God' of death, son of 'God'–'*Ra*'. Deemed 'Gods': they surpassed mortal men's stamina, stature and characters—revered giants.

'*Omniscient*' abilities: knowing everything in worldly existence, dwelt within. '*Omni–linguists*': understanding every language in Earth's hidden realms—natural '*polyglots*.' '*Pathfinding*' skills granted permission to track down people by closing eyes. Masters of '*morphing*,' they concealed themselves, camouflaging with their milieus. These beings often appeared invisible to the—naked eye.

Eyes change in the water. Three thousand feet buried beneath the secretive ocean floors, sixty feet mammoth '*Sperm Whales*,' swam smoothly gliding: stunning pulses at massive six feet '*Jumbo Squids*.' Navigating murky dark waters: tracking their victims, through '*Infrasound*.' Frequency vibrations sunk lower than 20 Hz (cycles per second) during this process, becoming inaudible to human ears. Elephants also possessed phenomenal hearing ranges, allowing them to eavesdrop on growling thunderstorms.

For centuries, cathedral organ architects exploited this phenomenon by utilising infrasonic organ pipes—inspiring a sense of awe in a congregation. Through '*ultrasound*,' bats navigated by detecting frequencies as high as *120,000Hz*, and dolphins *200,000Hz*. Extraordinary '*superhumans*' wandering 'Earth,' possessed—both these gifts.

Manifesting dreams into concrete realities through '*astral projection*,' and '*mental projection*': they could tap into their ethereal essence. Gifts of telepathy made these beings empathetic to all life—they felt everything. Travelling between worlds was their speciality. '*Cross dimensional awareness*' allowed them to detect affairs and advents in other dimensions. Defying gravity, like '*standing split*' (Urdhva Prasarita Eka Padasana) yoga poses—the sun shone on their—faces.

Full spectrum light frequency absorption granted them control over Earth's elements. These spirits had abilities to metamorphose into gaseous vapour-like forms. '*Animal morphing,*' dated back from ancient times. Mermaids – '*water spirits,*' derived from '*mere*': the 'Old English' word for '*sea,*' and '*maid,*' a woman. Goddess '*Atargatis,*' were the earliest mermaid tales emanating from *Assyria,* 1000 BC. Age-old mythology, portrayed mystical beings buried in the ocean's depths, magical creatures—resembling us.

'Fairy' emanated from the 'Middle English' word '*faierie.*' Stolen from 'Old French' '*faerie*': meaning: '*the realm*'—pure enchantment. Cast into ancient folktales: seen as guardians: '*tutelary spirits*'—small winged creatures who flew—over life's humps. '*Angels,*' held grandiose mysteries: deriving from the Greek, Αγγελος (ángelos), meaning: '*Messenger.*' Etymologically, Latin was the forefather of English, and Greek—mothered both. Ancient Greek and Latin poets often spoke upon mysterious beings—it filled literature.

'*Ovid*' (43 BC – AD 18), was a Roman poet who wrote the masterpiece: '*Metamorphoses,*' (transformations). *Ovid* Metamorphoses 8.731 ff:

"Some have the gift to change and change again in many forms, like 'Proteus,' creature of the encircling seas, who sometimes seemed a lad, sometimes a lion, sometimes a snake men feared to touch, sometimes a charging boar, or else a sharp-horned bull: often he was a stone, often a tree, or feigning flowing water seemed a river or water's opposite to a flame of fire." Proteus derived from '*protean,*' meaning: '*mutable.*'

Philostratus, Life of Apollonius of Tyana 1. 4 (trans. Conybeare) (Greek biography C1st to C2nd A.D.):

"Proteus, who changes his form so much in Homer, in the guise of an Aigyption Daimon . . . I need hardly explain to readers of the poets the quality of Proteus and his reputation as regards wisdom: how versatile he was, and forever changing his form and defying capture, and how he had the reputation of knowing both past and future."

Prolific Greek poet 'Homer,' wrote in Odyssey 4. 365 (trans. Shewring) (Greek epic C8th BC):

"Eidothea, daughter of mighty Proteus the ancient sea-god."

Greek mythology depicted 'Proteus': a *'clairvoyant'* early sea god—a forever changing creature.

Such magical beings existed on 'Earth' in 2049 AD: beings called: *'Wanderers.' 'Wanderers,'* endowed with abilities to create gaping black holes, creating swirling torrents of energy—opening portals. Accessing holes in the fabric of space through their minds—through solving equations. Known for travelling beyond light, they manipulated reality, breaking *'human'* boundaries—experiencing nature's indefinable.

"What's in a 'number?"

These beings possessed complete awareness of their true power. Understanding numbers: they cracked codes: unlocking dormant *'DNA strands'*—reclining in cells. Earth was a prison planet they felt: a distressing shambles. Opening minds became imperative, to escape Earth's grappling *'chokehold.'* Masters of language, they could decipher words to extract true meanings. Words emanated from numbers: sequences of words equalled to—specific number codes.

English contained infinite *'number codes.'*

"Why did *'Wanderers'* see Earth as a prison?"

Prison equalled the number of the word prism: *'prisms'* being transparent optical elements which trapped multicoloured rainbows of light. *'Wanderers'* talked of undesirable entities walking Earth. *'Undesirables'* captured the lights of children souls—their-imaginations. *'Undesirables'* sought to interfere with human number signatures. Every movement within our body produced a unique number signature. Every single emotion in the body emanated from a personal attitude. Chemicals were attitudes in the body, attitudes were numbers— they governed the world.

Clocks surround our world, keeping us in a stable state of perpetual fear. We are relentlessly governed through time: through *'numbers.'* Humanity has adopted a linear way of thinking: everything must have a start, middle, and ending. However:

"What if the end started at the beginning?"

Hard labour in jobs they despised, kept individuals at a particular vibration frequency—numbers were everything. Music vibrated on principles of natural harmonics. Eighty eight keys on the piano symbolised infinity, representing a star gate if you knew the—key—numbers. Certain musical frequencies could open the *'third eye,'*—pineal gland. Resembling a small pine cone, situated at the centre of the brain between the two hemispheres: great sages referred to this ethereal organ as—the *'seat of the soul.'*

Music comprised of numbers dancing in oscillations. Ancients believed hidden orders existed in music. They felt distances of celestial bodies from Earth corresponded to musical intervals. Ancients believed sounds, tones, and harmonics created reality. Music vibrations were measured in numbers of cycles per second *(Hz)*. *432 (Hz)* was seen as a universal sacred number frequency by ancients. Adolf Hitler, legislated standard tuning in instruments from concert pitch *A432* to *A440 (Hz)*. Subtle adjustments yielded unnatural rhythms, making us susceptible for mind control programming. Removing us from universal harmony: it left us nervous—unbalanced. Everything was orchestrated by immaculate design—aeons 'ago.'

Before letters, existed numbers: how everything in existence communicated. *'Earth's'* realm was steeped in duality—the great *'divide.'* Equalling number two: *'dual'* derived from Latin's, *'duellum,'* meaning, *'war'*: therefore, life would always be a bloody struggle—birthing all kinds of—characters.

'Characters' referred to people in a novel, play or film. Also a printed, written letter or symbol deriving from the Greek character: *'a stamping tool.'* Letters were characters wrapped in elaborate veils. Cracking

the code of a specific letter *'character,'* unleashed a hidden number—the letter's true power: its real—intent. 'Characters' shaped our personalities, particular qualities which defined us. Human beings referred to themselves as *'persons.'* 'Person,' derived from the Latin *persona,* 'mask'—character in a play. Actors reciting choral lines wore distinct masks in early Greek and Roman theatre. Mask emanated from Latin *per* 'through,' and *sonus* 'sound.' They spoke to the world, through—*'masks.'* Ancient Greek theatre was a ritual: a 'catharsis': Greek origin *kathairein* meaning: to 'cle anse.'

The *'Bard'* Shakespeare became famous through words: adding over three thousand words to the English language. *'Bards'* were literary poets, wordsmiths—number architects. *'Bards'* derived from the Celtic word *Bardos*. England's King James (1604) commissioned a council of fifty *'Bards'*—the country's finest. 'King James,' desired a uniform translation of the bible. The *'Royals'* controlled the *'Church of England,'* therefore the masses would be confined to the new bible. *'The Authorized King James Version'* became the soap the masses washed with: other versions were—strictly forbidden—fruit.

'Shakespeare,' was believed by minorities, to be indeed 'Sir Francis Bacon': editor, and word *'architect'* of first edition 'Authorised King James Version,' bibles.

'Old English' verbs and pronouns including: *'Ye, Thee, Thou, Shalt,'* were freshly introduced into English. 'King James' forbade 'Shakespeare' to publicise any involvements in the grand undertaking. However, 'Shakespeare' was an astute subtle word *'architect'*:

"How could he not leave his signature?"

Traces can be seen in the book of *Psalms 46:3* and *46:9*. 'Shakespeare' was 46 years old in the year 1611—the same year 'King James' published his bible. The *46th* word of the psalm begins *'shake,'* and the *46th* word ends—*'speare.'*

"How much of life is a coincidence?"

Intriguing number connections can be seen

throughout Psalm 46. 4+6=10: the tenth paragraph:

"Be still, and know that I am God: I will be exalted among the heathen, I will be exalted in the earth."

Counting six words, we see *"I,"* followed by *"am."* Another four words deeper gives us, *"will."* Reshuffling the numbers—6 and the 4, to 4 then 6 (46), we get—'William'—'Will-I-AM.' *'Bards,'* extraordinary *number wizards*, were renowned for leaving mysterious clues in strange places—hidden in plain sight.

Clothing revealed secret number codes—through 'architectural weaving.' People dressed to conceal themselves. Soldiers ('Soul'-dyers-losing souls through war), wore tanned green gray *'Universal Camouflage Patterns (UCP)'*: deceiving their enemies. Employers stuck in the busy corporate world, displayed *'status professionalism'* through: black suits, swanky ties, and rip-off *'Luis Vuitton'* handbags. Clothing consisted of intricate patterns. Every sound produced a pattern, which produced a form, which produced a picture. A famous saying goes:

"A picture is worth a thousand words."

Clothing represented pictures—indistinguishable from images to the eyes. If someone wore a spectacular garment, draped in a sea of rainbow gem coloured stones: many would likely be flabbergasted, exclaiming:

"Wow!"

Society breeds individuals inflicted with 'status anxiety': those wearing fancy apparels, to manipulate other's perceptions of them—a trick as it were. We adorn ourselves in words. Everything we wear is a fashion—statement.

A number was a symbol, a representation: letters were synonymous with numbers. The number code:

'1=AIL, 2=NZCU, 3=WEKM, 4=FHRXD, 5=S, 6=BG, 7=YTJUV, 8=O, 9=PBWQ'

Only nine numbers: from one to nine everything flowed, returning back into:

'1'

Numbers were formidable powers. 'W' equalled the number '3': the end of the twentieth century welcomed the *'internet'*—the web. *'WWW,'* allowed us to reach great heights. The three *'W's (worldwide web),'* equalled the number *'333': '3+3+3=9'*—the cycle of completion—signalling the end of an—'age.' A humongous paradigm shift occurred. Humanity had to decide, start questioning:

'Whether to hold on to a drowning ship? Or 'jump deck'—risk—everything.'

Crypto emanated from the Greek root word for secret. *'Cryptology'* was the art of 'decoding ciphers'—hiding intricate 'number data' in plain sight.

Earth *'Wanderers'* were unique master *decoders* and *encoders'*:

'Spell annihilators,' shattering time.

Daring to dream: declared—'Number Makers.'

WHO'S TO BLAME?

SYLVANNUS'S JOURNAL 2049, FEBRUARY 2ND

Maybe we only have ourselves to blame.

Our inherent nature only seeks gratification.

We seek to be seen.

Can we live in this world anonymously?

Free from a title or status?

Is it possible to remain nameless?

When did we begin to use judgement as a measurement of truth?

Can we really see beyond our projections, or do we only see our projections?

CHAPTER THREE

'PRAA SANDS'

THE four of us never worked. The day revolved around leaving our 'Earthship' spotless, to calm beach strolls, leaving footprints in pineapple gold sand. Pandora, fond of the sea, became more infatuated with finding recipes. *'Vegan'*– exceedingly healthy. Proteus branded her: a certified–*'health nutter.'* Perplexed, her staggering discipline levels confused him.

Pandora never consumed *'cooked foods,'* exclaiming they denatured enzymes: labelling them–*'pure poison.'*

"I don't eat to enjoy food, I eat to exist!" Pandora's popular house slogan.

Everyone agreed: microwaves were an unnecessary evil. Everything in nature spun to the right. 'Earth' spun from right to left on its axis, whilst revolving around the sun. Healthy cells spun from right to left. However, microwave molecules spun in reverse–from left to right–the exact direction of *'cancerous'* cells. Oscillating at wild speeds over 2450 million cycles per second *(MHz)*–microwaves cooked from the inside out. They produced life threatening, radiation–deathly *'carcinogens.'* Despite the wealthy plethora of health knowledge, Proteus still suffered intolerable cravings for 'devils pie.' When you have been dining with the devil for so long–eating without him feels–nakedly uncomfortable.

Well situated, 'Praa Sands' offered mind shattering panoramic views–illuminating the whole 'South West of Cornwall's' marvellous expanse. Equidistant between the jagged coast surrounding *'Lands End,'*: acclaimed for its ethereal beaches at *'Sennen,'* and the unearthly drifting estuaries of the *'Lizard Peninsular.'* Charming beaches: *'Falmouth,' 'St Ives'* and *Truro* were within half an hour's drive. Gorgeous 'rock pools' guarded *'Praa Sands's'* ends, like roaring lions.

Cornwall, world renowned for its brilliant surf, caught rip roaring 'Atlantic' swells: whilst picturesque landscapes smiled. Considered to be the best beach break on the South Coast, surfing season commenced from late autumn through spring—blossoming exquisite swells. Swells, referred to *'real waves,'* solid formations, generated through the wind blowing faithful over a large area of open water—the wind's—*'fetch.'* North easterly winds head gliding over 'Praa Sands,' created *'off shore winds.'* This was when the wind at surf breaks blew off the shore—a surfer's paradise.

By the coast several cafes, lesson centres, beach bars, body board and awesome surf shops—offered themselves warmly. 'Praa Sands' was *'nice,'* however, it was no *'Maldives'*: you required a *wetsuit*, preferably a thick black neoprene *5/3mm*. There were also abundant parking facilities located at ends of the beach. However, if you favoured calmer ambiences, then a small wander down the beach or through the roasted pumpkin sand dunes brought you downwards towards—*'Lesceave Rocks, Hendra,'*—barren even in the zenith of the season.

Protecting sanity, surfing allowed free roam of tranquil 'South West Coast' seas—alleviating persistent nightmares. Glancing reflections in crystal blue gold waters—I pondered unfathomable questions of—life.

Luz enjoyed cycling and catching winds. Nobody watched the *'holographic television'*: it told lies to your vision (tell-lie-vision)—telling lies visually. Instead, we preferred to embrace the nature's naked elements—staring into blue gold. Luz was a left handed, incense burning, alluring belly dancing, henna tattooed—extremely amicable spirit: full blown *'nymph.'* A sex fuelled modern society assumed *'nymphs'* referred to sexual derogatory connotations. Feminine principles were desecrated throughout *'western culture'*: butchered bloodily. Words retained clues: *'Pussy'*—vagina, *'Dickhead'*—penis, *'Asshole'*—anal orifice, *'tit'*—breast. Over ninety per cent of curse words in the English language, referred to sexual organs in demeaned manners. 'Nymph' derived etymologically from Greek *'numphe'*—veil: female deities in ancient Greek mythology: divine spirits of nature in the forms of beautiful young women.

Pandora exuded flawless beauty: keeping healthy not only by food, but through stretching to immeasurable lengths. Extending well pedicured toes, flexing arms, bending legs, twisting fingers, curving spines, straightening spines, titling her head: yoga helped her defy gravity, to be anti-gravity. Practicing daily, Pandora instilled within my bones her favourite mantra:

"You can't rest on your laurels!"

Laurels were plants with dark green glossy leaves. Interlocking leaves of the 'bay laurel' formed laurel wreaths. Awarded as the accolades at the 'Delphic Games,' honouring the Greek God 'Apollo': laurels being his symbol. Laurel trees arose when nymph 'Daphne' metamorphosed herself into a laurel tree: chased by Apollo's hungry pursuit of her. 'Daphne' derived from the Greek word for 'tree.' The 'Delphic Games' were one of the four *'Panhellenic Games'* of Ancient Greece: the precursor to the modern Olympic Games. Every four years, sanctuaries in 'Delphi' offered 'Apollo' homage. 'Apollo' spoke through the Delphic oracle: the Delphic maxim—*'Know Thyself.'*

Proteus lost himself in his guitar, playing with a hearty passion. Luz accompanied—humming along—strengthening her soul. Guitars were based on number notes *(A5-G3-D7-F3-B2)*: similar correlations could be seen within monetary notes. *'Currency'* alluded to a particular monetary value—units of energy. Everything in existence contained currents: therefore, the currency (money) we worked for was in actuality—ourselves.

Playing his guitar taught Proteus the secret 'elixirs' of life. He observed the powerful abilities of the muscular and nervous system throughout the body. His body remembered and repeated movements they experienced. The bedrock of our whole learning processes in life operated through—*'muscle memory.'*

Cells within the body contained memory. Proteus realised, whatever his fingers experienced doing in those states of total relaxation—they did at lightning speed.

Training his whole body in this manner, he realised the human body was more miraculous than we could ever imagine. Music was similar to rolling waves, modelled around tension and release: rests and peaks. Proteus became intimate with his fingers: developing—*'total body awareness.'*

Pressing wrists into the face of the guitar created tension in muscles involved in the playing process. Specialising in the *'Floating arm'* and *'Light Finger'*: Proteus moved his fingers across the guitar—like a butterfly. The *'Light Finger'* was the completely relaxed finger brought to the string: touching the string with only the weight of the finger. The 'Floating Arm' was when an arm held its own power and weight, supported by a relaxed body. Proteus's fingers were energised through *'intention'* and *'attention.'* Deep sensations lead to the—ultimate feeling. Proteus: the *'Wizard,'* received this nickname, due to paying incredible attention to detail. Proteus was aware of every single breath. Breathing is essential to live, everyone breathes, but not everyone breathes deep—enough.

The air permeating our 'Earthship,' contained *'Himalayan herbs'*, *'Sandalwood'*, *'Astasuganda'*, *'Saffron'*, *'Ambergriss,'* and other medicinal ingredients. Pandora and Luz cherished incense, burning it until we fell asleep. Luscious dark aromas slyly engulfed our cores, tranquilising us. Pandora always sought new aromatherapy oils and waters. She adorned her smooth soft hazelnut butter skin with *'Geranium Organic Floral Water,'* which she described as:

"The glow from the 'Gods"

Born with two dark dazzling beauty spots, on the top corner of her right eye—Pandora took care of herself. She felt all women should embrace their femininity, nurture their wombs. She often graced her well formed toes with *'Cold Pressed Camellia Carrier Oil.'* Pandora beautified herself incessantly, however, never became anxious if her hands acquired dirt—an uncanny paradox. She was no perfectionist: finding it absurd – humans beings strived for perfection, whilst in nature they were no straight lines. She would tell us, emphasising each nuance:

"Perfection is a curse: a spell you have to break. We do not walk in straight lines, we walk around in circles: round and round we go."

Laughing to pieces, Pandora was hysterical—witty with a wicked sense of humour. The four of us cherished each other's company: moments shared together were—pure euphoria. Staging pretend comedy shows in our *'Earthship,'* amused us—life was a laugh. Each person took turns exaggerating their alter egos, exposing sides of themselves, laying them bare. Leaping into wild dancing states in dazed frenzies: absorbing the bizarre absurdity of our life existence. Laughing became necessary: the harder we laughed, the better. We laughed, until lungs clapped in applause.

Bed times were not fixed: we would stay awake for a whooping twenty-four hours straight: yapping away like adventurous school children—defying the wrath of their parents. Time was of the essence. The past, present and future appeared to roll into one—seemingly. Always the first up in the morning: I had lots to plan. Some saw me as a leader, but I was not. While shepherds watch their flocks by night: I was neither a shepherd nor a sheep: I followed—nobody.

'So where did that leave me?'

Living in the city left me isolated—alien. Expending precious energy heedlessly: caught up in a barbarous game: a contest where I knew not the rules. No manual, only coffee stains on my white linen shirt. *Mary Shelley's* Frankenstein had been reborn. Traipsing around, trying to tender testing temptations: addiction—my disease.

"Relaxation is what we are: stress is what we think we should be."

Dissatisfied, my body transformed into a ravished corpse: an inanimate carcass. Worms of the worst kinds proliferated within, eating my guts from the inside—out.

"This can't be life?"

Reams of traffic cramped my mind, bullying me. Traffic lights only showed me stark bright red. Stationary, running tired feet on below zero *'Norwegian ice'*: slipping, sliding—dying. Baggage bundles slept underneath eyes, without paying rent—like a bunch of cockroach squatters taking chance. City life filled my stomach with floating butterflies: it made me feel—queasy. Small intestines were roaring seas of acid. A hyperventilating hypochondriac: a shabby mess, shoddily shaking: shuddering, shivering: staggering searching: shimmering blood, cooked inside—the heat was on.

Writing, the only remedy: the panacea which cooled the red hot molten lava soaking my veins. Communicating through words, numbers, symbols: observing unique patterns of 'letter architecture'—words cured. Writing taught in depth 'alchemy'—metamorphosis. Using lead from pencils to create worlds of grandeur: painting giant waterworks on canvases invisible. 'Alchemy' derived from the Persian *kimia, 'Elixir'*. The Persian could be traced to Greek *khemia,* 'art of transforming minerals': which in turn traced back to the ancient Egyptian word *keme* 'black earth.'

Ancient Egyptians (Kemites) referred to alchemy as 'the science of change.' Chemistry was also the mystery of change (mistry). They witnessed the miraculous transformation of 'black soil': it was forever changing forms: birthing rainbows of colours. Everything came from the darkness: born though the womb's star gate: born drenched in amniotic fluids: the darkness held—great mysteries.

Words were mysterious creatures, whose exact origins would remain forever veiled. Words being thought producing chemicals: served as languages of communication throughout the body. There were no facts in life—only interpretations.

"What does this word mean to you?"

Nobody ever read a word in the same way. The ancients were aware of 'the power of the word.' Words were numerical calculations, wave oscillations vibrating at different speeds—depending on the intent bestowed upon them.

"Sticks and stones may break my bones, but words will never hurt me!"

I disagreed. Words could kill a once healthy individual, in a matter of seconds. *'Spells'* were words: *'spelling'* being one of the oldest forms of magic on Earth: the most virulent kind. Positive intentions through words levitated minds to the highest degrees unimaginable.

Marcus Aurelius's *'Mediations,'* changed my perceptions forever. Intriguing life philosophies furnished pages: reflections of life: contemplations: ruminations: deep thoughts of introspection, sails into uncharted waters.

Writing my journals began ten years ago: random personal occurrences: diaries consisting of puzzling questions, life-affirmations: fuels for 'alchemy.' I wrote until the ink bled, until the lead starved itself in sacrifice to the page. The quest for knowledge became my preoccupation: hunting down rare ancient texts—lost scrolls. Nothing could cure my insatiable hunger. A mouth barren dry like *'Safari desert heat'*: knowledge became water quenching arid cells: resuscitating membranes, pouring life into them. I became an unstoppable wisdom lover.

Philosophy, meant love of wisdom. Greek *philos* 'loving': referred to liking a specific thing: *'philology.'* Greek *philosophia* 'love of wisdom': Sophia Greek Goddess of wisdom.'

"What do you value most?"

Freedom became my only goal: I would fight, until hands were battered, worn to the flesh. Life still hung in the balance. Unresolved issues lurked near like contagious coughs: uncertainty invaded my blood, but I refused to lose.

"Give fear the upper hand? You must be joking!"

Deadly *'Chimeras'* crept into my dream space: a marvellous inception. Grotesque fire breathing monsters, consisting of fierce lion heads, wild goat bodies, and venomous serpent tails. Nervous nights produced nocturnal numbness. An insomniac caught in a gruesome tug of war: my body—the rope. Breaking into cold sweats: water gushing from my back—enough for a bath.

"We live in the world we think of."

A marvellous secret I stumbled upon. All is mental, our mind carries—us.

I have observed society divide men and women on the basis that they will never understand each other. I have witnessed this godforsaken cancer rise to abominable excess. Permeating humanity's pores—saturating them. Soldiers die unnecessarily in a blood bath of wars, nightmare brawls. Every film billboard poster bears an image of a gun, why?

"How does this subliminally trigger us for warfare? What does this do to our children? What will they become?"

I watch as humanity reduces itself to a perpetual state of childhood. How social milieus continue to contaminate the minds of the youth. Religions separate man farther than our closest star. Rituals put us in trances: routines regulate us. The womb of the planet bleeds profusely, while we continue with the same robotic customs—afraid of change.

Hierarchical structures invade humanity's consciousness like decaying plague: like wild bacteria over one hundred and twenty degrees, replicating—refusing to chill. Pharmaceuticals lie to the masses: they only lead them to the gallows—the gates of hell. They tell you they're nearer to finding cures—they lie.

Masses wait for the world to end: riotous: praying their violence might bring its demise sooner. We have dumbed down to such a degree, we feel intelligent. Eyes are strained—retinas damaged—we cannot sleep. We butcher animals mercilessly for their flesh:

"Who will forgive our actions?"

I wrote to challenge beliefs, to question everything.

'Numbers Makers' possessed power because they never ceased to question. They were rare to find: they found you. Known for disguised appearances, they would have to reveal themselves to us.

We were approached by a 'Number Maker' last month: a random stranger on the beach. He carried a friendly charm: we arranged to meet next month. Scanning his aura, Luz sensed a unique spirit of sorts. We counted down days: patiently waiting—spellbound by this mysterious—soul.

FEAR IS DEAD

SYLVANNUS'S JOURNAL 2049, FEBRUARY 12TH

Fear is dead!

Fear is a self-created feeling, activated by cellular memory.

Fear is when we are afraid of what might potentially happen.

There is always a possibility, never an outcome.

There are no new fears, all fears we have are actually one ultimate fear.

Fear can never be new or different, because it is from the past: it is based on memory.

Fear is never in the moment: only in the thoughts we have about the moment.

We fear forthcoming events and people, because we do not know them.

When we suspend our judgement, the fear dissipates.

Fear is like an old man waiting to die.

Fear is dead—love is alive.

CHAPTER FOUR

THE APPOINTMENT

"A MONTH PAST"

WE met him by the seashore. His name was Gothlin: an aged man with a youthful shine. Jet black dreadlocks descended – kissing his knees, resting against his frayed rumpled orange topaz robe. Self-assured, relaxed jaw muscles: a face of exuberant energy. His ruler straight spine brimmed with confidence, as he pulled his shoulders back–arching his back. Holding his head high, tilting it upwards: his neck muscles relaxed. Words emanating from his chest added powerful bass to his voice. Speaking: pausing: creating anticipation within us–rushing words not his style. His body relaxed –calm. His immaculate diction exuded crystal clear clarity. Maintained eye contact throughout our entire conversation, left us–speechless.

"Questioning keeps me young," he told us, speaking in deep tones, gesturing, deliberating whilst speaking.

Ever since adolescence, human nature fascinated him: how we changed. Living in over thirty countries: arid deserts, arctic ice, violent sand storms: he weathered environments which would leave the majority of us wearisome.

Gothlin considered himself neither prophet nor sage.

"Tune into the elements," his only message.

Comprehending disturbing realisations at age fourteen, becoming conscious, cognisant of 'Earth.' Knowing too much, too young. Dreaming more real than reality: downloading infinite streams from occult sources. Overwhelmed by knowledge: unwrapping gifts–curses. Teased throughout childhood: labelled '*crazy*.'

'His burden?'Knowing secrets—being chosen.

Reluctant clenched fists, lips shut forming tight lines; symptoms of an abandoned child's growing pains.

Seeking to fit in: normality his goal, he strove for sanity inside a mad world—hoping to dissolve inside mists of anonymous clouds. Living in London, the city of opportunity; the world became his stage.

Dormant gifts gathered thick dust, atrophying. Resisting harnessing gifts; he began to lose them. He became a mere mortal. Suffering for his actions; he rode the bumpy *'Wild West train'* to annihilation. Begging on weary knees for redemption's grace; his consolation: he still dreamt in—numbers.

Ten years remembering, returning to his core. Rekindling old flames; distant childhood memories; his energy was re-awakening. Embracing disowned gifts; he vowed never to blink again; to remain forever awake—his journey had begun. His lifelong quest revolved around understanding hidden secrets of the universe; unlocking number codes. A long tiresome, strenuous journey. Riveting adventures around the world, observing how numbers worked; how they affected us—all.

He studied until eyes closed on books. Questioning his reality, leaving no stone unturned: learning dark esoteric secrets; forgotten arts. He became aware of the function of numbers. Numbers served two purposes on Earth: they comprised of the tools to count and they helped to understand the baffling; unexplainable.

Gothlin realised the ancients constructed *'The Great Pyramid of Giza'* through numbers. Perfect proportions throughout nature created beauty; patterns of symmetry; proportion being the mathematics language. Influential Greek philosopher Pythagoras (c.580 BC – c.500 BC) believed all life began and ended with numbers. Convinced they held keys to life and death; he studied them. Pythagoras travelled to Egypt (Kemet) and Babylon in the 5th Century BC.

Acquiring ancient knowledge of right triangles and sacred numerology, he became credited for proving *'Pythagorean Theorem.'* Pythagorean Theorem stated:

"In any right triangle, the sum of the squares of the two right-angle sides will always be the same as the square of the hypotenuse (the long side). A2 + B2 = C2."

Secret knowledge of numerology and right triangles originated thousands of years before in ancient *Sumer* (Iraq). Minorities believed people of ancient *Sumer* gained this knowledge from ancient astronauts landing on Earth around 6000 BC. The secret knowledge then passed to the Babylonians, which in turn passed to the Egyptians.

'Mystery schools' throughout ancient Egypt taught supreme universal laws: Pythagoras became an initiate. Upon returning, Pythagoras settled in the city of Crotone in Southern Italy, teaching the sacred sciences. His philosophy around mathematics inspired those close by. Developing a following of upper middle class politically active students: a select circle formed, known as the *'Pythagoreans.'*

Immortality their quest, they sought to perfect physical form to acquire immortality. Believing divine providence governed us, karmic wheels of reincarnation. Disciplining the body: freeing themselves of base natures: fearing returning to 'Earth,' to re-learn the same lessons. Puritans, they avoided meat and beans: living by strict codes of law governing all aspects of life. Believing souls would only be saved through accumulated merit: they strove for vibrations of eternal harmony. The *'Pythagoreans'* were called *mathematekoi* meaning:

"Those who study all."

Mathema is the root of the 'Old English' *mathien,* "to be aware," and the Old German *munthen,* "to awaken." A wealth of knowledge overwhelmed Gothlin: becoming empowered beyond measure, he began cracking number codes.

Noticing unique number patterns and infinite similarities: he saw certain patterns displayed within numbers, contained the very patterns of life—itself.

Observing different shapes illustrated in flowers, fruits, plants and trees:

'His revelation–' they all possessed different number codes.

Ancient Greeks studied the *'golden ratio'* existing in all things. They saw the 'golden ratio' in everything: from vortex formations of matter, to biological systems, onwards up to solar systems and galaxies. The Greek letter phi (φ) became the initial letter of Greek sculptor Phidias's name: a symbol for the golden section. (φ) Expressed itself in the pyramids of Egypt, the Parthenon in Athens and European Gothic cathedrals. Used by artists and artisans throughout the—ages.

Gothlin studied the science of attraction, what made men attracted to women: symmetry is beautiful. But there was more: when two people contained equal numbers, they began to see each other: they began to surrender. The human face is an example of divine proportion. The head forming a golden rectangle with eyes at its midpoint: the mouth and nose placed at golden sections of the distance between eyes and bottoms of chins.

The beauty unravelled further. The golden section consisted of four lines in a perfect square: from the pupils, to the outside corners of the mouth. Viewed from the side, the head illustrated divine proportion: ears reflected shapes of 'golden spirals.' Golden smiles display *'golden sections.'* Teeth form golden rectangles with the front two incisors, with a phi (φ) ratio in the height to the width. The ratio of the width of the first tooth to the second tooth from the centre is also phi (φ). The ratio of the width of the smile to the third tooth from the centre is phi (φ) as well.

Ocean depths held dolphin secrets: their eyes, fins and tails, all fell at 'golden sections' of the length of their bodies. The number secrets lied—everywhere.

Handwriting displayed *'Golden Proportion.'*

Whilst writing, we placed horizontal bars in capitals (upper cases):

"A E F R B H P"

The horizontal bar, divided the letter into a larger and a smaller part, forming the *'Golden Proportion.'* Once Gothlin remembered his essence, he became—invincible.

Contemplating gnarled folds of walnuts, watching them mimic brain appearances.

"A body softer than fruit?" Seemed so.

Fruits correlated to the body. Slices of carrots to iris patterns; pomegranates' chambers to hearts; grapes to lungs; avocados to ovaries; figs to testicles; ginger to stomachs; mushrooms to ears; kidney beans to kidneys. Throughout the ages—great lies were told.

Imbuing masses with fear, symbols became curses—the pentagram. During the Christian inquisition, inquisitors believed any non-Christian obviously worshipped Satan; therefore the symbol became synonymous with devil worship. In the purge of witches, the pentagram became named the *'witch's foot,'* bearing evil connotations: how things—change.

The *pentagram* symbolised the *pentad*; the pentad symbolised five. Symmetries of *pentagrams* existed in us, the body's inheritance; resembling the five senses; sight, hearing, smell, touch and taste. Symbolising invulnerability, the *pentagram* became a magic tool to ward off evil; mirroring the five toes and fingers. An ancient Egyptian *hieroglyph* (sacred carving) for the *'underground womb'*; it symbolised the maternal womb—coming from darkness into light. Pythagoreans considered the *pentagram* the symbol of perfection. They labelled points of the *pentagram* with letters:

U: Hudor=water

G:Gaia=earth

I:Idea=form/idea

EL: Heile= sun's warmth=heat

A: Aer=air

UGIEIA translated into *Hygeia,* meaning health or divine blessing. *Hygeia* became the Greek Goddess of health: her name a common inscription on amulets. Forbidden fruit in the form of apples, when cut through—revealed *pentagrams.*

"What other secrets lie in the garden?"

Nature inspires us, from there we draw symbols: from there—we see everything.

Gothlin explained: numbers governed reality. Nature dictated through numbers. He assured us, if we understood their workings, they would—set us free. He told us, we exist in one of three realms at any moment. There existed realms of creativity, realms of balance and realms of destruction: he saw all—dying more than once. His metamorphosis opened—his eyes.

Studying mathematics in schools and universities: he noticed they were counterfeit. Strategies devised to veil the real power of numbers, attempting to dissuade us from further study. Gothlin said knowing their true significance, would make us masters—*'Gods.'* Giving us abilities to create any technology we chose—in a matter of seconds.

"Every single piece of technology has been created by Number Makers," said Gothlin.

"Aeroplanes, telephones, automobiles, radios, computers, architecture: you don't feel they got here by accident do you?

"We have come a long way since then. Now we create what you cannot see—things invisible. From the genesis, time has governed us: calendars, numbers. Humanity's insecurity caused their fall. Existing on a planet we knew nothing about, trusting foreign entities for guidance. Praying these entities would care for us: they only enslaved us—further.

"Foreign entities created illusions through architecture, vast labyrinths: worlds within worlds. Distinguishing authentic worlds from fake ones became challenging, even for the greatest of minds. Cast under a spell, tricked. Foreign entities understood numbers, they took advantage of them. They acquired power, dominion over all kingdoms on—'Earth.'

"Fair or unfair, moral or immoral.

"The universe far exceeds our petty ideas of right or wrong. Earth is stranger than we assume: an endless maze—unknowable," said Gothlin.

Gothlin continued sharing his history (his-story). Telling us specific thought forms were engineered to control what we thought. Thoughts were boxes, not our own, but someone else's. He stated every single thought form produced by the brain emitted number frequencies. By everyone thinking alike, number frequencies could be better monitored. In other words our days were—numbered.

As long as thought forms operated in the consensus reality, we ran risks of being controlled. He showed us the poison food had become: how food became weapons of warfare used against us. By masses consuming filth, foul polluted junk, they switched—off.

"Vibrating low frequencies produce the same numbers, it's all about the numbers: you can play their game, or create your own," Gothlin said.

He witnessed drug disasters and alcohol fuel global societies. Humanity restrained by bandages: distracted: desensitised: comatose: beggared beyond belief. Lulled into further states of amnesia: cast into realms of—forgetfulness.

"Humanity has not arisen from its cocoon," he bellowed.

"This is my destiny: what I came here for, let us proceed:

"How many seek to embark on the great journey?"

"Only the four of us," I replied.

"Only four?" Gothlin said, smiling with a deep glow.

Proteus asked more questions than I, becoming

curious how the process worked. Kindred spirits, Pandora and Luz listening in an awesome wonder became more curious. Both connected to the divine feminine flowing through their veins. Using intuition, I sensed they trusted him. They seemed relaxed, strangers of this magnitude seldom entered the midst of our presence; it humbled us. Pandora focused on Gothlin's animated lips, keeping internal logs for every word echoed. Pandora mastered the art of memory—total recall.

"So could you please tell us how these portals work?" Luz asked in a shy, high pitched voice.

Remaining quiet for the entire conversation—questions tormented her.

"Oh, the portals" laughed Gothlin, with another glowing smile.

VENTURING THE DEEP

SYLVANNUS'S JOURNAL 2049, FEBRUARY 14TH

Upon venturing the deep, one realises—the deeper you go, the deeper it gets.

You go so far down, until eventually you forget from where you came.

All I know about reality is what the media tells me: it will only change, if I question it.

Whatever we see, will always be subjective: for a camera can never see greater than its lens.

These current institutions exist because we need them: when we no longer need them, they will no longer exist.

We are paid to keep this system going, so why the hell would we want it to stop? If we wanted it to stop, we wouldn't be doing our—jobs.

Not everyone came to Earth to learn the—same lesson.

CHAPTER FIVE

THE DISCOVERY—DARING TO DREAM

SINCE 2013 AD, Earth portals were officially found in every country in the world. The information lay in the public's hands, made accessible to all. Research findings were well documented: conducted by the famous Dr. Sebastian Jacques Pingo, and his research team –'Everest.' The discoveries made Dr. Pingo an overnight celebrity: receiving tumultuous international praise—volumes of press recognition.

Science was steadily becoming the new global religion. Altars in Dr. Pingo's name filled homes: the masses worshipped him. Dr. Pingo's research team 'Everest,' discovered similar peculiarities on every major land mass around the world. Their findings showed specific landmarks contained powerful energy grid lines. These grid lines were unique, emanating special energies. All major grid lines around the world were published in a report in 2015 AD.

The report entered the public domain, surfacing on *'Blotix'*: the new internet. Dr. Pingo called these unique areas *'Portals,'* because they opened doors to infinite possibilities: they lead to other realms. His research team observed, certain individuals when placed on these portals, showed something startling. Recording energy levels through specialised energy devices: he watched energy levels quadruple when certain individuals stood barefoot on the *portals*. Great mystics throughout the ages knew the power these portals held—they made pilgrimages there. However, science demanded proof—not fanciful fairy tales.

The masses craved tangible evidence, something they could put their hands on. Ancient peoples built monuments of grandeur on top of the sacred portals, placing stones on unique grid lines. From the *'Great Pyramids of Giza'* to *'Stonehenge,'* giant monoliths stirred humanity's imagination—they inspired hearts. These powerful sites left us questioning the ultimate of all questions:

"Is this it? Or is there something more powerful beyond us all?"

People often reported out of body experiences when visiting certain ancient sites. Old records and accounts showed people felt lighter in body, as if they were defying gravity. Dr. Pingo and his team coined this phenomena—*'Floating with the Gods.'* This was due to individuals losing all consciousness, appearing temporarily dead. Individuals remained stationary until they choose to come back—down to reality.

Few possessed this unique gift. Before Dr. Pingo arrived on the scene, the pre-existing medical establishment labelled individuals undergoing such experiences. Those portraying symptoms of wild delirium, excessive convulsions, those appearing to suffer from repeated seizures. They labelled them: *'epileptic'* and left it there. Things have changed drastically since then, science woke up: it had no—choice.

'Nephron,' was Dr. Pingo's main energy recording device: this sublime machine, measured subtle fluctuations in energies surrounding the portals. Referring to it as the: *'master computer,'* it weighed over two tonnes—a pure beast. He became fond: *'Nephron,'* revealed many secrets, calculating numerical values on screens, showing energy levels varying: rising and falling. Dr. Pingo would rub his dry hands through his thick beard, smiling as—the numbers changed.

He had been interested in number sequences since childhood having been born to the son of an architect. He was aware of the *'Fibonacci sequence'*: how certain shapes produced certain numbers—sacred geometry. This sequence was named after the Italian mathematician *'Fibonacci,'* who lived during the 12th century. Fibonacci was educated in North Africa, where his father Guglielmo, held a diplomatic post in what was then called *Bugia* (today called Bejaia): a Mediterranean port in northern Algeria. The Fibonacci sequence occurred in nature, modelling the population growth in rabbits and also the development of the spiral in a snail's shell.

The terms in the sequence could be made by adding the previous two terms:

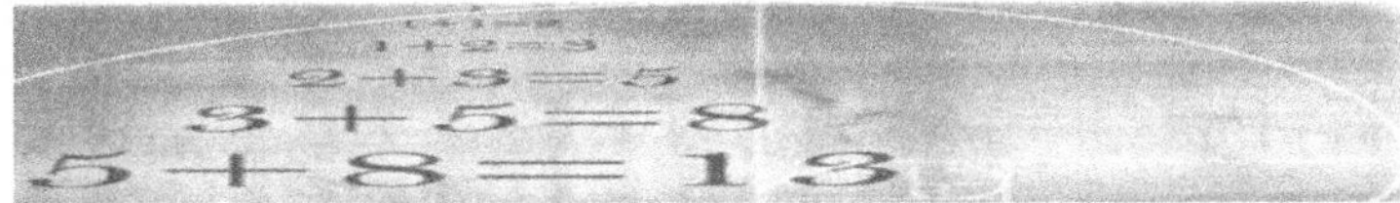

"What's the difference between a pentagon and a square?"

His father used to tell him the only difference were the numbers: nature was vast codes of numbers. By cracking number codes, one would be very powerful indeed. Dr. Pingo exhausted himself researching, until puffy swollen eyes touched his thick glasses. This is what he lived for, what life was based around. His earliest findings showed him the extraordinary power of nature. He knew his findings would shake the scientific world, if not—shatter them.

Dr. Pingo and his research team sampled entire world populations: they gathered individuals from diverse backgrounds: hundreds took part in the unique study. Certain participants in his research, altered *'Nephron's'* number volume so significantly, he labelled them: 'Number Makers.' He sent away private lists of each compelling finding to governments around the globe: information would be stored in secret databases—for further investigation. Governments viewed these unique few participants as valuable assets: searches of background histories being already underway.

The deal: Dr. Pingo would be financed by certain governments and in turn they would receive all significant findings. They granted Dr. Pingo free reign, access to all portal sites around the world. The research project required ample resources. We were gradually living in a world where people saw falsity in money—only resources interested us. Dr. Pingo received access to abundant resources, all expenses taken care off—with ease.

Imagine a human being produced an average Power Generation, of a hundred watts, on a daily basis. The *'Power Generation'* permeating these portal sites, reached over two hundred and forty mega watts of electricity. It would take one hundred and forty turbines to generate and equal that amount and provide enough power for one hundred and fifty thousand people or—more. Now you see why these great monuments have captured hearts and imaginations for so long; it's as if we inherently know their true power.

According to Dr. Pingo, 'Number Makers' were strange people—natural geniuses. From time to time, thoughts crept into his mind. Reflecting on the 'Number Makers' in quiet moments, he felt they held certain answers; clues to nature's mysteries. Life on other planets formed the basis of many conversations; it was no secret—we were not alone.

From time immemorial, chosen families travelled to the stars. They not only visited moons, they journeyed to other relatives in distant galaxies. Earth lagged behind; its technology compared to other stars—primitive. Earth had devolved immensely. Other planets used far more sophisticated technology. In the beginning, the human body was the *original technology*; however upon entering realms of deception, we gradually relied on more—external technology.

The production of technology on Earth was strictly controlled. Every year we received an upgrade, but it was the same; it had all been planned out a long time ago. Our planet traded with neighbouring planets for centuries. We gave them what they wanted, they gave us what we needed—a mutual exchange. The technology we used was decrepit; other stars possessed technology more than one thousand years ahead of us, floating in space—airborne.

Earth spacecrafts never travelled the stars — that was a hoax; a governmental experiment. Scientists used 'Number Makers.' Number Makers were endowed with abilities to open portals—star gates. These beings could travel through time. Science was aware time was an illusion, a man–made concept, devised to enslave the masses.

No two human beings were the same, even if they appeared to be. Extraordinary beings dwelt amongst us: beings classified as—*'Superhuman.'* Described as time travellers because they could travel through time they could morph into different life forms at will—bending time.

The ancients became fascinated with stars, seeing them as reflections. Accustomed to seeing beings appearing half human, half animal: the ancients were in awe of life's diversity. They filled literature with stories of these strange mystical beings. Viewing them as not from this dimension: they called them—*'star travellers.'* In reverence they named constellations after them: they can still be seen throughout the—sky.

Modern humanity has forgotten its essence, casting itself into deep slumber. The world is not your friend. We separate ourselves through religion, race, gender, class, hierarchy and social status. We destroy our foundation and expect a stable house. The havoc began thousands of years ago and the *spell* was cast: now we run around lost—with no compass.

Magical beings labelled in mythology as fairies and angels were the *original time travellers*. These beings possessed abilities to fly through dimensions: their symbol became *wings*. Angels could fly only because they took life lightly: they were not of this—world.

There was no good or bad in the universe, only consequences. Certain beings crossing realms made pacts with 'Earth's' early scientists. Promising to show them the world beyond: to fly them to other worlds: and they did exactly as they said. Science kept information hidden for centuries under wraps. A strategy not to usher in public uproars: people always feared—what they had no control over. Dr. Pingo knew 'Number Makers' could do exactly the same. He knew his research team could fly with them: however, only 'Number Makers' chose who they flew with—you required permission. Number Makers held the last word—they held the keys.

'Number Makers' could open portals through numbers. Excited, Dr. Pingo realised the tremendous possibilities lying ahead: however, finances dwindled. He had exceeded his time scale. Due to lack of resources, he abandoned all further projects. Hitting like concrete, Dr. Pingo felt the blow: worse still, his *'hypotheses'* were not proven. Speculation flooded the air to whether or not portals existed. Governments labelled Dr. Pingo, *'a new age lunatic,'* blasting his research: claiming it held no scientific validity.

Dr. Pingo's intentions were noble. Realising what the world was, he saw its true potential. Suffering blood, sweat and tears to bring information to the forefront: however, he was stopped in his tracks. Dr. Pingo dreamt for humanity to realise: nothing was what it seemed. We were living in an artificially constructed reality with—blinds pulled over eyes. He admired the brilliant scientist Nicola Tesla: a true mastermind. Nikola Tesla paved the way for modern technology. Tesla realised by harnessing energy from Earth's electromagnetic field, we could have as much energy as we desired—free energy.

Dr. Pingo received worldwide press coverage, showcasing his ground breaking research: however—it was not enough. Burning urges engulfed him. He would not rest until his findings spread full scale – he wanted the whole world to know. Governments became uncomfortable with releases of Dr. Pingo's findings to the public. World leaders felt citizens would become poisoned by hearing such information. Receiving copious death threats—the second assignation attempt proved—fatal. Touring 'New London,' he gave several press conferences promoting his new book—*'Imagination.'* He was scheduled for 'New York,' to conclude the tour: he never—arrived.

Dr. Pingo heard the door of his Baker Street apartment crack wide open. Blood rushed to the top of his head, he knew who it was. Defiant body muscles tightened: he sat on his bed—unflinching. Sweat oozing from his brows, crawled into his mouth. Waiving arms uncontrollably, to resist the gagging—he fought the hardest he could. Tired lip muscles attempted to break free, from thick black tape. His breath became troubled, panting—gasping. His head knocked around the van, heading towards 'London Bridge,' like a bunch of—conkers. Squinting eyes to see: there was only—darkness.

Dr. Pingo's heart raced as they bound his feet together. Suspended in thin air for a split second: his stomach felt—woozy. Only a silent insignificant splash could be heard, as they tossed him head first, over 'London Bridge.' Buried deep under cold water, as wet as a fish—forgotten—they silenced him.

Tributes poured throughout the world, everybody felt his loss. It was a public shock: he was on the verge of marvellous discoveries. After his death, nobody talked about Dr. Pingo like they used to, but we did: we still—dared to dream.

Conversing with Gothlin on the beach was a privilege. Overwhelming us with information: he gave us more than we could handle. An original participant in Dr. Pingo's research experiment: he showed him everything: now it was our turn. Gothlin began explaining about the *portals*: we soaked up every—word.

"So why did Gothlin want to help us?"

He said, it was his duty to show humans other worlds: other realities. He never asked for anything from us in return: only that we would not lie in telling what we saw to others.

'Tryathon,' was one of the endless planets the 'USA' (*Universal Space Agency*) had discovered. They officially reported thirty three new planets in our solar system. Gothlin told us there were far more: there were as many planets as there were grains of sand.

"Infinity!" bellowed Gothlin, raising his hands:"infinity, only infinity."

"We are all Number Makers," explained Gothlin.

"We do it all the time, through our thoughts. We create geometry with our thoughts, our projections create our reality. Thoughts are children—take care of them."

He said, he was able to travel to these planets through his mind; creating them through his thoughts.

"Imagination is a marvellous gift, when you know how to open it," he said smiling.

"They exist within me; when I travel to them, I travel within; reconnecting with the true self."

Hubble telescope shots of Tryathon showed freshwater lakes and enormous rock like formations. Mysterious liquids were found, submerged in deep waters; they appeared to be—crystals. Marine life also existed and other mammals including—wild bears. Even extraordinary dragonflies were sighted. Gothlin said: in ancient times, many humans fled 'Earth' to live there. The ancients were great seers, they realised what the world was becoming. Earth was just one of the many airports in the solar system. Beings from other galaxies came here; however, many overstayed their visit.

"Wide arrays of unclassified life forms wander amongst us; Earth is full of mystery," said Gothlin.

Earth's current world population in 2049 AD soared to over twelve billion. '*Speed pregnancy*' technology allowed women the luxury of '*instant babies*.' It was a technology created by English scientist Brian Anderson. The technology worked by speeding up '*Embryogenesis*'; a process by which the embryo formed and grew, until it developed into a fetus. Gothlin never believed the published figures of twelve billion to be true, or by any means—accurate.

"You have no way of knowing how many people there are on 'Earth,' unless you count each one. We say twelve billion because it's what they tell us, but they don't know anything, they know—nothing!"

screamed Gothlin.

Gothlin realised the *'Undesirables,'* created generations of mindless consumer and through highly advanced programming techniques we were being–played.

"What makes a human being so powerful, they need to be distracted, abused and put in state of perpetual fear?"

"Someone knows who we are," said Gothlin: "they know what we're capable of."

Gothlin assured us he could open the portal to Tryathon: warning us to prepare ourselves – many died in its roaring oceans. Bowing heads into the palms of our fingers, we grinned, our time was—now.

SHATTERED GLASS

SYLVANNUS'S JOURNAL - 2049 MARCH 1ST

Truth is like a glass shattered onto the world: everyone picks up a piece.

Life gives us all the ingredients to make whatever we want out of it.

The meaning of life is what you make it.

What the soul truly wants, the soul shall truly find.

The owl does not ask the Eagle, who am I?

It knows deep down and follows its own path.

"Oh, God laughs at us!"

CHAPTER SIX

"HOW DID WE FALL?"

SMELLS from the kitchen seduced stomachs as we sat at the table. Buckwheat, plantain, falafel, iceberg lettuce and *'Thai'* long green beans—filled plates—we ate well. Smiles illuminating our faces brought us closer together: making us thankful to be alive. Staring across the table, I watched flashing sparkles in Luz's eyes. Silent attractions developed between us. Palpating hearts—increased pulse rates: widening pupils—frozen breaths. The glow grew brighter, warming us. Testosterone and oestrogen meandered arteries, like wild rivers. Thoughts of sharing kisses entered our minds. We leaned forward: however, never crossed—the line. Our eyes followed each other—casting us under *spells*. A divine representation of the womb: she did a marvellous job.

Quality time spent with my mother gave me everything. Her only wish was for me to respect women—to cherish them. Loving my mother only made my affections towards women more intense. Birthing a star: I owed her everything. No man is greater than their mother. Feminine energy is under threat, on the verge of utter silence: it lies in jeopardy.

"How did it come to despise its reflection?"

Men and women live disconnected from each other: we lie with foreign bodies, whilst making love. Strangers to ourselves: we see each other as opposites. Men and women our natural complements: women being looking glasses for men to see power, men being looking glasses for women to see beauty:

"So why war?"

Women strive in today's society to fit in, to gain power: competing with males to their own detriment: there is great power in—vulnerability. Women thought they should be ruthless and insensitive, whilst living in a man's world. Stereotypes associated with masculinity only sought to destroy the planet further. Over centuries, women sacrificed wombs, to no avail: crucifying them, and in return—they received a phallus. The wounded womb, scarred all over, resembled 'Earth's' condition: a mirror reflection.

Distaste for women, distaste for all nature. Who sees the face, does not see the heart: a glamorous culture. Blinded by the lights, we accept superficial realities: mistaking them for—universal truth. And the clock ticks: the battle between men and women must end—before we do.

Small minorities of women viewed themselves as an embodiment of the *divine feminine*. They saw themselves as goddesses. Luz and Pandora, were two such women: they knew their greatness—we all did. They added airs of marvellous freshness to our home—beautiful fragrances. In times, when humans were becoming more and more isolated: I counted my blessings, to be in the presence of such brilliant minds. No man is an island: I remembered the saying from childhood. The four of us needed each other—we existed as a whole.

Throughout human history, Earth has been depicted as volatile.

"People are dangerous!"

Mass propaganda spread cancerous viruses, infecting us. They portrayed Earth in negative lights, forgetting its beauty. Labelling us as dangerous wild animals: filth, which needs to be controlled. The media told us we were flawed in more ways than one: forgetting to tell us the one.

'Trust nobody, the message for—today.'

As a child I was told not to trust strangers, but I never questioned why? Now I realise they could never give me answers which would suffice. They too were running off fear indoctrination programs: they were parrots.

Growing up, I ate the healthiest foods and dressed in the finest clothes. Born into a household flowing with harmony: my mother through her kindness, showed abundance was our natural birthright.

"How many children are born into a world, where no one cares? Why have children, if you cannot care for them?"

I pondered these questions. I never liked school, but I never let it interfere with my education. I was always finding ways to improve myself: it was not about—fitting in. I only had one opportunity at this: I was not going to—blow it.

THE NEW INTERNET-TECHNOLOGY WARS

'Blotix,' the new internet helped us connect with the wider world. News feeds were uploading and updating every minute of the day. A fresh news feed surfaced on 'Blotix,' showing rebel fractions assembling themselves within the city. 'New London' was under siege, under hostage: under arrest. The rebel group called themselves: *'Winds of Fire.'* Proclaiming the city had become unruly: they claimed it needed to be tamed. Apparently they knew what was best, they knew what we needed. Armed with highly sophisticated lasers: they replaced the old fashioned fire arms with guns. The fate of the city was uncertain—treading on unbalanced tight ropes.

Officers patrolling streets flashed lasers beams, decorating city apartments, night and day. They guarded the city like queen chess pieces: illustrating power at any given opportunity. Wearing thick black metal toe cap boots, weighing down feet: they held lasers in tight grips. Lasers were subtle weapons: the new war had become—silent. *Lasers* were engineered for 100% pin point accuracy: they never missed their target.

We received another news feed through 'Blotix,' reading:

"Anyone who does not abide with the new law will be taken out."

In 2049 AD, news statements became blunt, razor sharp: they never minced their—words. Tronan, lead the rebels: they respected his commands. His rise to power in the works since 2020 AD meant he saw himself as world emperor, divinely chosen—by the *'Gods.'* Buried deep in his plush 'Mayfair' mansion (West London), he gave orders, smiling. There was a heir of arrogance to the way Tronan moved around his mansion—he hunched his shoulders, his eyes focused on himself.

Oblivious, masses never knew Tronan was sponsored by a neighbouring planet: a distant star called: *'Neptis.'* A star which had vested interests in Earth: what it could offer them. Tronan received the latest technology, the best 'Neptis' could offer. The technology was new to Earth, but old from where it came. We lived in the digital age, future wars would be fought through—technology.

Transportation on 'Earth' changed with the onset of the technological revolution in 2012 AD. The 'X-matron,' the future car of 2049 AD: wired to emotions, self-recharging whilst driving: an intelligent design. Under water diving capabilities: self-changing paint colours: regulated high speed—the first talking car. Possessing abilities to hover over traffic: inbuilt flotation devices: surveillance cameras and holographic windows. Self automated *'X-matrons,'* governed themselves through autopilot: programming themselves. Functioning via remote control: we could control them from the comfort of our homes. These savvy machines became the preferred method of transportation in the city—accompanying the—*'Blue trains.'*

'Blue trains,' the trains of the future, boosted efficiency. The gauge changeable trains used gauge changeable bodies and gauge changeable rails, to run on different railway tracks. 'Blue trains,' changed the distance of the wheels on both sides automatically after passing the guide rails: therefore they could run on the rails with different gauges. 'Blue trains,' ran at super speeds through powerful magnetic forces, from super conducting magnets. Conventional trains in London ran on the rails with wheels, whereas the *'Blue trains'* floated and accelerated at super high speeds of over *1000 km/h*. Running along side roads: they travelled from North West London to Central London in close to three minutes. Citizens named them 'Laser trains,' because they were so–damn fast.

London's architecture kept growing: they built buildings out of nothing–creating them in our sleep. In 2045 the city changed its name to 'New London.' Building upon building emerged in the city, dwarfing us like ants. Tronan imagined 'New London' to be the city of the future. London etymology derived from the word *Londini*: translating to 'the temple of Isis.' The Romans named the city 'the temple of Isis,' in reverence to the Egyptian Goddess Isis. Paris also derived from Egyptian *per Isis*, 'a temple to Isis.' Paris translated into 'large temple to Isis' *(Per Isis)*. England once had been called modern Rome, due to its global conquests. Tronan planned for Rome's resurrection: its revival.

The time arrived to embark on new conquests: ones far more ruthless. Tronan possessed technology for world domination, it lied in his hands. His forces prepared thoroughly for the takeover: equipped for war. They were aware slow resistances were building: however all challenges would be dealt like flees–sprayed to death.

Nephli, wife of Tronan, stood by his side in all matter of affairs. Chosen during childhood she was selected to be his loyal faithful servant. Responsible for masterminding 'New London,' she guided Tronan's military strategies. Her charms infected the public–her beauty froze them. Wearing elaborate dresses, she left spectators dazzled–hypnotised by her splendour, capturing city hearts and minds: winning public–favour.

THE CITY'S BREW

Meanwhile from 'Praa Sands,' we could smell the city's brew: the putrid aromas. It was written, there would be hard days ahead: we just never thought it would be this soon. We had to counteract Tronan's oppressive regime: stop his bacteria, before their tentacles spread any further. Using force to combat Tronan's dictatorship would be futile: we would be crushed. Tronan specialised in warfare: torturing people. His forces already shot dead several people in the streets with lasers. Equipped with super technology, they acquired resources to control whole nations. This served to be a warning to us, a lesson: an example of what happened to foolish individuals attempting to spoil their—plans.

"Our hearts cried out to 'Tryathon,'" they screamed. Technology existing there surpassed Earth's by light years. The pre-existing ways of life on Earth continued for too long: masses were ready for change. There were steps for travelling through portals to stars. Upon entering 'Tryathon,' purification was necessary. Accumulating grime and grease throughout the day: clothing layers covered pores, blocking us from—real feeling. Only water could cleanse our auras: water could—replenish us.

Having fresh salt water flowing outside our home made us aware of our blessings. Sea salt contained crystals: full of micro elements and minerals, it fought against infections. Sea salt was a natural *antihistamine*, which could be used to relieve asthma. Salt helped to flush mucus and sinus congestion, also preventing muscle cramps. Water, the great healer, tranquillised us.

Hydromancy derived (from Greek *"hydro"*, meaning water, and *"manteia"*, meaning divination): was a way of divining by means of water. Ancients healed themselves by staring at water, ebbing, flowing—rippling. We had opportunities to dive into infinite waters whenever we chose. Luz's eyes sparkled every time we mentioned 'Tryathon': she encapsulated all of our excitement.

"Can you imagine when we are finally there?" she said.

Clutching her soft palms, I smiled, replying:

"We already are."

The four of us conversed in the presence of a burning camp fire, outside our 'Earthship': we pondered the language they spoke on Tryathon.

"What if they have no language," whispered Proteus, laughing. A natural joker, he kept us all entertained. Pandora adored him, they shared a special bond.

Pandora mastered the English language: she created architecture through words. A *multi-linguist* speaking five languages fluently: her passion emanating from childhood. Her mother was adept at understanding the etymology behind words, their hidden meanings: passed the divine knowledge onto her daughter. Pandora was forever telling us about the mysteries of languages.

"English is spell language," she said. "The word grammar derived from the word *'grimoire.'* The *'grimoire'* is a book of *spells*: a textbook for magic. When a child goes to school, they learn how to *'spell.'* English is encoded with double meanings. The words are dipped in trickery, tricks to—confuse us."

She told us language used in law was a tool implemented to mask words—obscure their true origins.

"When people say good morning, they cast spells unknowingly," said Pandora. "The brain cannot distinguish subconsciously between the two words: *morning* for the day, and *mourning* for funeral. We are really saying—*good sadness*.

"Grammar are the *spells* which govern language: laws are the *spells,* which govern us," Pandora said smiling.

We shared information with each other on a

daily basis: it was healthy for the soul. We needed to question everything. Life teemed with endless possibilities: it would be shameful not to see—what was possible. Word imagery had always been used to trick how we decoded reality. The only way to control was through the mind – trapping imagination. Through our five senses, we experienced reality: they were our decoding mechanisms,

"But could we trust our senses? Who was controlling them?"

'Praa Sands' helped our metamorphoses. Luz adored walking bare foot on the sand, while water passed through her naked toes. Calm silences, tranquil breezes: we had all the time in the world. Upon awakening, I echoed the mantra:

"Start the day well and afterwards, see what happens."

ENTERING TRYATHON

Proteus drank his coffee, while stroking his lover Adriana's arm. She joined us for lunch every Friday: the only time she had off work. Proteus spent hours teleconferencing Adriana in Salvador, Brazil. Digital relationships through *'Holographic communication,'* became part of world culture. 3D digital images of Adriana often appeared in our living room. Almost human, but not quite: she never looked—real enough. I maintained digital friendships with people in: New York, China, Ethiopia, Russia and Brazil—a global connection. This was the future—virtual people in your living room.

Proteus *'The Wizard,'* loved new breakthroughs in technology: it offered him freedom. He stayed up late, eyes fixed on holograms, weary eyed.

'When you don't work, you're not afraid if you don't wake up.'

Friday never meant the end of week for us. Time was an illusion, we never counted in days. Saturday was like any other: we saw the sea and it had not disappeared. While waking to perform her yoga, Pandora stumbled across a crumpled note by the side of her bed:

"Meet me west of ocean, Gothlin."

'Pengersick Castle': a code name for *"West of the ocean,"*: happened to be one of a few portals in England. *'Pengersick Castle'* was a fortified Tudor manor house hidden away in 'Praa Sands,' between *Helston* and *Penzance*. The oldest part still standing dating from 1500, but there had been a building on this site for at least 900 years. Reputedly the most haunted castle in Britain: it was built on unique energy grid lines. Accounts showed people had disappeared—labelled lost. The castle was temporarily closed to visitors.

At last, the time came: the four of us hurried at once. Our pulses increased tenfold, this is what we had waited for: now it was upon us. The short fifteen minute stride from 'Praa Sands' beach never flustered us. Upon reaching, we felt the immense energy permeating the castle. Gothlin stood outside the castle: he lived there. His facial expression signified the magnanimity of what we were embarking upon.

"You will be Number Makers," said Gothlin. "There will come a time, where I will no longer be relevant to you—where I will no longer be needed."

Pandora straightened her feet, as we formed a tight circle. Bowing his head, Gothlin positioned himself in the centre. He began chanting foreign words, making us feel eerie. Holding out a transparent sceptre, he raised it, before smashing it to the ground. Ripples of light began forming: blinding us. Bright lights surrounded us, blurring our vision. Gothlin kept disappearing intermittently. Lifting his head, he turned to us:

"What do you seek?"

"We seek Tryathon," said Proteus, full of audacity.

Gothlin burst out laughing.

"Many have said the same: scientists, doctors, lawyers, teachers; businessmen; priests; I could help none of them. They were untrustworthy, conniving crooks. A magician must never show an onlooker his secrets; in case they become him. People have offered: vast sums of money, cars, mansions, but this world could offer me nothing. Government ministers have pleaded; Kings and Queens, begged; I refused. They were not ready; they had ulterior motives; but I have seen through your souls, they are pure. Not everything is to be revealed to those asking.

"I must warn you of the great dangers involved in crossing realms; the waves do as they choose."

"We understand," said Pandora.

The hall began flooding, as water from castle cracks and crevices poured forth—tides of water gushing at us.

"Fear not," said Gothlin.

Pandora gasped for air, as freezing waters threatened to drown her.

"I assume you can swim," said Gothlin.

Luz's flapping arms and kicking feet struggled to tread the violent waters. Gothlin dived through the waters; we followed behind, ducking heads beneath below zero temperatures. Gothlin swam through a hole at the bottom of the castle hall. We swam behind him through the hole, until we vanished. We remained traceless, even our bodies had changed—composition.

A THOUSAND

SYLVANNUS'S JOURNAL - MARCH 4TH 2049

Shame on the man who thought he knew:

For he died too quickly,

Trapped in his shell, unable to break free.

Taken captive by his own fear,

His cup full, his mind fuller,

Shame on the man, who thought he knew—for he died too quickly.

A thousand voices, but which one is mine?

A thousand smiles, which one was true?

A thousand laughs, but which one was genuine?

A thousand tears, but which tear is the true water from the soul?

CHAPTER SEVEN

WELCOME TO TRYATHON

LAND OF THE NUMBER MAKERS

LUZ kept swimming until our bodies entered a vast ocean. Spewing waters from my mouth, I watched them hit the surface—rippling. Stranded in the middle of nowhere, only roaring waves and wet bodies. Swimming to shore, we glided through the waters with ease; our bodies weightless.

"Where were we? Were we dreaming or in reality?"

There is a thin line between the two. Intuition through sensing confirmed unanswered questions—Earth was light years away. Pitch darkness greeted us, almost resembling a womb. Our eyes became blinded, in the midst of the darkness—obsolete.

Altering our physical make-up; we were now ethereal in composition. Feeling lighter than ever—thoughts of flying crossed our minds. The darkness intensified further, as a warmness swept through our cores, filling our ethereal vacuum; the sun arose within us all.

Sudden streams of light in Gothlin's shape emerged. Following him further, we witnessed something profound:

"Gigantic mountains of caves stared at us."

We made contact: vast caves, billions of them. Star flies hovered above our heads, glimmering in seas of bright lights resembling x-rays. Fluttering crystal transparent wings, their glow remained impeccable; a turquoise greenish blue. What felt like a second, lasted an eternity. Peering from the rock like surface, we crouched so nobody could see us; staring in fascination; marvelling at Tryathon's sheer awesomeness.

"Welcome to Tryathon," said Gothlin.

Breathing sighs of relief permeated the atmosphere, engulfing it. We crossed realms: Earth becoming nothing more than a distant—memory.

"You will meet many beings here: none will do you any harm—fear nothing," he said, turning to us.

"How many times have you made this crossing?" Luz asked, facing him.

"Too many: I was born here," replied Gothlin, smiling.

Pandora and Proteus became more nervous, than I'd ever seen. They knew there was no turning back now: we'd already committed ourselves. Still awestruck, becoming overwhelmed by the grappling scale of our voyage: sights left us frozen: the landscape—phenomenal.

"How would they perceive us? Would we make it out of here alive? Would we ever see our lives the same way?"

Too many questions, but deep down, we knew all would be revealed—in time.

Suddenly, a shadow of light appeared behind us.

"I am Hathora, welcome."

"Uh...I am," I said stammering, struck by nerves.

"Don't worry," she replied, "I know everything."

Her appearance resembled our own. But there was something more: a deeper intrigue, I could not quite fathom.

"I will be your guide," she said in a bold voice. "If there is anything you need, do not hesitate to ask: it's been a long time coming."

Fixating on bright *streams of light* emanating from her core: we became mesmerised. Pinks, blues, reds, yellows—colours we'd never seen. Turquoise shallows emanating from her eyes added to the marvellous ambience. Turning her back to us, she began whispering:

"I take many forms, what you see of me, is not

me. This is only what you are allowed to see, at this stage. As we venture deeper, you will see me in different lights. I know the plague that besets Earth. We watch you from here, we were once there.

"We understand your struggle. We watch how you create meaningless wars; how you enslave your own kind; how money governs your reality. We see billions of people still under the *spell*, cast so long ago. Earth is sick; however, do not be alarmed; she is in metamorphosis. Everything must go back to its origin—you cannot escape from what you are.

"Inhabitants of Tryathon exist in your dreams. The *streams of light* you see are torches; to show you the world beyond. Infinite numbers of beings dwell in Tryathon; I have not met every one. None has ever harmed me; each sleeps in its own element. There is no time in Tryathon, only movement. Age does not throw itself at us—we are what you once—were.

"I remember travelling your planet light years ago, she was bountiful. Gothlin tells me, she has still not changed her ways; she is still—forever giving.

"In the beginning duality never existed, no competition; no separation. Everything moved in divine motion. When divine rain impregnated her dry Earth, life sprouted. Admiring her infinite creations, seas of voices began forming. This was the way she communicated with her creation—how she spoke to them.

"She gave birth to giants, dwarfs, animals—anything your mind can imagine. Coming from her, she was the source—the originator. The wind was her flute and as she blew trees—flowers moved. Scattering herself in the water and land; her essence permeated everything in existence. After completing her cycle, she gave birth to the *'Originals.'* Emerging from soil; they were the first—aspects of her mind.

"Beings from other galaxies arrived in swarms to Earth. Breeding with the *'Originals,'* they produced offspring. Their children contained two polarities: abilities to create and abilities to destroy. Every star possessed a unique signature; Earth's being free will which allowed the *'Inbreeds'* to perpetuate themselves—in this—ridiculous manner.

"The land of milk and honey became transformed into the land of chaos and hell. *'Originals'* became enslaved by the *'Inbreeds'*: by beings resembling them, but which were not. Earth became an experimental laboratory, a distressing testing ground. Throughout the aeons, great wars were fought between the *'Originals'* and *'Inbreeds.'* This affair was neither good nor bad, there was no such thing in the universe: there were only—consequences.

"The *'Originals'* once served as conduits, working through universal mind. This was all before the great disconnection, before our imprisonment. During their zenith, the *'Originals'* constructed grand monuments, elaborate skyscrapers: buildings today's modern architects can only describe as—unexplainable. By living in sync with the universe, nature protected them. The *'Originals'* received their nourishment straight from the tree—and the tree served them well.

"The *great disconnection* arose, when the *'Originals'* fell asleep. Relinquishing sovereign powers, they became prey—targets for those wanting to deceive. How it was then, is how it is now. The *'Originals'* still fight for their freedom: they still fight for their—voices to be heard.

"I hear the screams from Earth: screams of a billion prisoners: screams of abandoned children from their mothers: What have we become?"

"We have seen Earth disintegrate into a handful of ash. We watch your master manipulators create famines, debt—prisons to house you in. How they create endless languages, to keep you divided. We watch the *'Undesirables'* perpetuate false claims: a myriad of lies. A world full of screens, lots of squares, no circles. Tryathon has seen it and we will watch no—further.

"Tronan receives his technology from a close star to Earth—*'Neptis.'* The *'Governor of Neptis'* has had vested interests in Earth, dating back, as long as

I can remember. They seek to conquer her, make her theirs. In the age of technology, Earth is starved of wisdom. Soulless beings crawl your Earth, they plague it with sickness. The battle is for the hearts and minds of the people: a mind monopoly. We have more to talk about, but first let me show you around," said Hathora, hovering over us.

WANDERING TRYATHON

Perplexed by the mind shattering knowledge, we followed Hathora further through the strange land. Everywhere we looked: we saw *streams of light*. The immense colours:

"Who was their architect? Who created all of this?"

"Here, you will only see light streams: there are no bodies. The body is only a vehicle: a transporter. Light streams act as our vehicle—our casing," said Hathora.

"Inhabitants of Tryathon continue to help 'Earth,' whilst her population threatens and destroys itself. Numbers of beings have risen to incalculable numbers. Infinite creatures live inside Earth—monsters you never knew existed. The universe contains many versus: great seers described it is as: *a giant hologram*. Our lives are nothing more than a drop in the ocean. There is no end or beginning, only what you see around you—a hollow void.

"Masses have been conditioned to believe everything must contain a beginning and an end: however, Tryathon only hears the constant sound of the universe—its eternal hum. We do not believe in illusions of grandeur: belief has no place in the universe—we either know—or we don't.

"Inhabitants of Tryathon seek to enter 'Earth's

realm again; we are ready to fulfil the prophecy. Tryathon possesses technology Earth once had: *'original technology.'* We access it by tuning into ourselves, activating our authenticity. The secret is: our minds are portals—deep star gates. Developing *'original technology,'* allows one to become a 'Number Maker'—architects of their own reality.

"Every piece of architecture is comprised of numbers; a specific code. On becoming architects of your own reality, you will possess abilities to rearrange numbers—unlock codes. We are familiar with 'Earth's' expression:

"Thinking outside the box."

Stepping outside the box makes the box smaller, until eventually it vanishes. This is how we 'Number Makers' work: starting off small and then expanding. Inhabitants of Tryathon are 'Number Makers,' because we build—infinite realities.

"Earth cannot be changed by force. People will always possess choice; however, we can remind Earth, of its greatness. Not every star you see in the sky shines for you. Many use your light, to receive their glow. There will be wide resistances, upon entering your *realm*; masses will cling to old routines—fight for them. Tronan will be awaiting us; beings from *'Neptis'* will have informed him. Many casualties will arise from this war—much blood spilt. But fear not, everything returns to its origin—nothing is lost," said Hathora, glimmering in seas of lights.

Remaining mute, we drowned ourselves in calm silences which purveyed; our words carried no weight. Hypnotised from Tryathon's allure, time ceased to exist; becoming nothing more—than a lions stride in eternity; miniscule.

Our *appetites* were tamed, ever since we entered the *portal*.

"Nobody eats here," Hathora said, flashing beacons of light.

Neither one of us were certain if we were still

breathing. Perhaps this was all part of our imagination — Gothlin's magic trick. The mind is a maze, which the best of us can lose ourselves. Thin streaks separate what the mind can conceive, to what turns out real. We never questioned the authenticity of Tryathon. This planet was no less real than our Earth experiences—it was all a dream.

Time came for our departure. Gathering us, Gothlin headed for the *water portal*, as we floated behind. Hovering towards the vast ocean, mysterious *light bodies* brushed against our sides. *Light beings* over 300 feet beamed down lights—illuminating us. Focusing on us, we watched their bodies move—like sheets blown by hot summer winds. We stared into the ocean: psyching ourselves for the grand crossing. Throwing ourselves towards gushing waves—we buried bodies below its freezing cold surface. Gliding through dark waters, nothing became visible—only darkness. Pandora's waving arms formed spirals in the water—incredible patterns. Submerged within deep waters, lived a plethora of luminescent sea creatures. Proteus felt intense warmth from bright lights—reflecting off his core.

Drawing out his transparent sceptre, Gothlin waved it through the crashing waters: as our bodies jerked back from surging shock waves. Bulky waters weighed our bodies down from all sides. Luminescent sea creatures scattered, as troubled waters shook back and forth. The waters took on funnel shapes—moving, compressing, expanding—twisting. Cold waters began creating massive swirling vortexes: our cores becoming sucked up from the vicious hydraulic. Pandora's hair spun 360, as we lost ourselves inside the fierce waves. Cold waters pressed against us, as we whirled round and round. Limitless lights enveloped us, before total gloom—blackout.

The waters decreased velocity, slowing down our thumbing pulses. Crystal clear glassy waters emerged. Proteus's lungs screamed for air, as his arms and legs thrashed wildly through the waters. Extending hands, Luz reached for him, but his body drifted off: carried by the—powerful currents. His tears mixed with chilled waters, as blood froze. Crippling circulation, stiffened leg muscles—his facial muscles lay motionless, paralysed from the shock. Numbness swept through the back of his spine, making vision blurred. Seeping to the depths of his throat, waters denied him permission to speak. Trembling lips, gagged for air. He struggled to maintain consciousness, as his mind headed for hollow blankness.

Proteus's scleras revealed themselves, as his irises wandered to the back of his cerebral hemispheres. Cold waters soaked his body, taking refuge: pulverising guts like sharp razors. The more he struggled, the more disorientated he became: up, down, left, right—nothing made any sense anymore. He pushed with his arms and legs, but he could find no leverage. For all he knew, he was pushing himself further into the abyss. His lungs burned for more air, and even though he knew he would get none—his body still took a breath.

Cold water trickled down his lungs and blood pounded behind his eyes. Sheer desperation: Proteus moved his fatigued hands—reaching out only to grasp the nothingness of the infinite ocean. Blood vessels in his eyes burst, fading to subtle black. Distant calls from us could be heard in his failing ears, but message signals were inaudible. The darkness engulfed him and he had nothing left in him to fight anymore. He surrendered and let the waters—take him.

Racing towards the *'Atlantic Ocean's'* surface, Gothlin carried Proteus's empty shell in his palms. Sunshine gazed upon our faces as we focused at 'Praa Sand's' golden coast— we were worlds away. Fresh smells from salt water filled the air, invading our nostrils. We saw the usual surfers riding waves—laughing, smiling: throwing hands up in frustration at—missed waves. Our mutilated arms, front crawled until we reached the shore—our prayers were for Proteus.

Gothlin carried Proteus's water filled body onto the sand.

"He will be fine," said Gothlin, "give him a day of good rest!"

Coughing and murmuring, Proteus sipped in and out of consciousness—the game wasn't over. We shared mixed feelings concerning recent events: the verdict was undecided:

"Should we abandon dreams of Tryathon?"

Crossing realms fulfilled the dream, to see the world beyond: however, there were prices to pay upon new ventures. In an eyeball blink, we returned—doing the unimaginable—travelling between worlds.

Tryathon made us remember, we lived in a flash of—light.

LIKE ATTRACTS LIKE

SYLVANNUS'S JOURNAL - MARCH 7TH 2049

Every creature is attracted to that which resembles it.

To possess something is to become a slave to it.

Your hardest trials will come when you feel you're weakest.

What you feel is your weakness, may be your greatest strength.

Your thoughts are your children—take care of them.

I know as much about people, as I know about the world: not very much.

Fear breeds complacency.

He that is on the ground need not fear the fall.

Life is the eternal story, because you never know how it's going to end.

I know too little about life to draw conclusions.

Humanity's story is told within its art.

You truly do not know yourself, when you depend on someone else to tell you who you are.

What you fear becomes your God.

I'm tired of making what's already made.

There is no battle, so drop the sword and take off the body armour—for nobody can hurt you.

Superheroes and villains—I am both.

Your greatest adversary is also your—greatest friend.

CHAPTER EIGHT

TASTING WATER

TRYATHON showed us endless possibilities: the true potentialities of our existence. Welcoming us with open hands: the trip made us see lives in different lights. 'Number Makers' would soon be descending upon Earth: it would not be long until they joined us. This was the last straw: we knew this time in Earth's history, everything would be—revealed.

Heading straight for the fridge: Luz poured a glass of fresh mineral water, before gulping it down. Tasting water on her lips again: a sublime joy. The four of us sat in the living room with silent stares: feeling an awkward numbness—shocked from our bizarre experience. Observing something peculiar—time remained still. The clock's hands stood in the same position—unflinching.

"It's a miracle!" yelled Pandora, gobsmacked. *Light streams* still clung to her body: she still looked—ethereal.

Entering unto 'Blotix', I checked the latest city updates: there was always news, monstrous news. Bulletins showed Tronan deploying more rebels into 'New London's' jammed streets. Insisting and maintaining public order was essential—for the sake of our own good. *'Blotix's'* news feed reported more city dwellers losing lives in horrific rebel clashes. More bodies were found slumped in rotting sewers—the city's madness. This type of news became normal, a summary of city life: fast and furious—nothing unexpected.

Tronan incorporated *'Hegelian'* philosophies to maintain law and order. 'George Wilhelm Friedrich Hegel' (1770–1831), was a 19th century German philosopher and theologist who wrote The Science of Logic in 1812. He developed a system called the *'Hegelian dialectic.'* This tool served to manipulate humanity into a frenzied circular pattern of thought and action.

The framework guided our thoughts and actions into conflicts, which lead us to a predetermined solution. The Hegelian dialectic shaped our perceptions of the world, helping us manifest visions for the future. This old model still served its purpose in the 21st century: problem, reaction, solution.

Tronan created problems in the city: the masses would react and then he would solve them. Going the extra mile—he gave us no problem, imaginary threats: we would react and then he would solve them. Possessing all the answers, he knew what 'New London' needed. The only way to stop: the privacy invasions, expanding domestic police powers, land grabs, insane wars against inanimate objects and outright assaults on individual liberty was to step outside the *dialectic*. This released humanity from the limitations of controlled and guided—thought.

Creating problems throughout the city guaranteed Tronan instant power—more problems—more rule. Every powerful dictator needs a problem, otherwise there would be nothing for them to do. They need our—power. People running the world never worked, they supervised: the greatest law makers, were the greatest law breakers. Living in fear delivered power to those—protecting them.

Roaming his Mayfair mansion, Tronan took robust strides—asserting power at any opportunity. Viewing dictatorship as destiny: being chosen from birth—picked to govern men. Initiated into *'The Circle of Trust'*: a secret society protecting Earth's hidden truths. Learning by age thirteen about 'Real Earth,' and its occult treasures. Studying forgotten buried scrolls—tablets explaining how Earth became a—prison planet.

"So above, as below."

Understanding this old principle of the universe: Tronan realised distant galaxies lived in war, they also spilled blood. Hierarchical systems created on Earth only reflected larger realities. Hierarchies existed worlds beyond us—an endless food chain.

His wife Nephli also became initiated into *'The Circle of Trust'*: knowing certain secrets, but not all. Both offspring from chosen families—their lives were mapped out before they were born. Chosen through bloodlines and genes: cut from a different cloth. Nephli would dance over Tronan in bed, exposing her *coffin tattoo* resting above her navel: a mark from the *'Governor of Neptis'*— his symbol for death. The Governor fed off war, humanity's blood: purer blood—providing greater sustenance. Favouring children's blood due to its crystal constituency—the great chain of events unfolded.

"We ate animals for nourishment, but did we ever ask who consumed us?"

This was the genesis, how humans came to find themselves in great chains around the globe. Possessing something they desired, humanity's burden emanated from those seeking to live forever—by any means necessary.

In ancient times many beings from star *'Neptis,'* travelled Earth, bearing gifts of supreme technology. Showing the first few magnificent secrets: teaching hidden *number codes*—how to unlock Earth's *doors*. Once you understood numbers, you understood it all. With numbers you could build whatever you wished—create mazes upon mazes. Architecture comprised of numerical codes: our foundations—built upon numbers.

Chosen families shown the supreme technology, made deals with these beings—signing pacts. The Governor used them as pawns in the game—powers of control always existed higher up. The Governor knew the divine power of the *'Originals,'* he knew they were immortal. He devised plans to harness the *'Originals'* infinite power: to make their energy serve him. Inhabitants of *'Neptis,'* sought to conquer Earth, to govern it. Before they could do this, manipulation was essential—universal mind control. They could never physically control everyone, so they created mental prisons instead—uncomfortable habitats.

Chosen families growing powerful beyond measure became: rulers of lands, kings, queens, priests—emperors of dynasties. They formed *priesthoods* and different *schools* of thought. Knowing secrets of the universe, *'The Priesthood'* kept masses blind. Building mazes and grand labyrinths around the world, their plan—for us to never find ourselves. By not sharing the divine wisdom of the universe, ignorance reigned supreme. This was their goal: a population of drones—mindless automatons.

Wreaking further havoc, *'The Priesthood'* began altering polarities—deleting the feminine principle out of life's equation—robbing Earth of its womb. A universal law illustrated: *'the law of gender'* throughout nature. Everything in nature contained masculine and feminine principles, reflections of the whole. Other laws in the universe also governed us. Invisible laws: strict codes were present—even in our denial of them.

'The Priesthood' were first to rule over humanity, becoming heralded as *'Gods.'* Holding them in high esteem, masses paid them homage. Gifts of thanksgiving filled temples built in commemoration. Mythologised: becoming the best loved characters in—humanity's story.

The high science *'The Priesthood'* understood was *'Originals'* never died. Through trickery, they kept masses distracted, amused and entertained. Telling masses time was short, to live for today—eat, drink, be merry—humanity's motto. Cheering us to indulge raging passions: bearing smiles as we dabbled further in buffoonery. Festivals and special days of celebration were created, to honour their names. While masses partied, they planned: *'The Priesthood'* knew otherwise—they knew better.

Knowing through their children they would become immortal, they groomed them in different fashions. Separating them from the herd, they initiated them into secret orders. Holding on to threads of power required reproducing offspring in their absolute reflection. While masses self destructed, they sought new ways to tighten grips of control. They understood the nature of the game, after all—they created it.

Blaming *'The Priesthood'* for Earth's fall would be foolish. Humanity's naivety played its part, insecurity causing their own demise. Humans sought someone to worship: while they worshipped themselves. *'The Priesthood'* labelled themselves: *'The Power'*: 'The Ambrosia,'—*'God's Cream.'* Working hard, day and night, to keep secrets hidden, buried forever. Even until this day, sweat trickles from their brows: they know they're days are—numbered.

It's only a matter of time before their pipes burst: nobody stays on top forever—even those who feel they should be. Throughout the ages, *'The Priesthood'* spread empires across vast lands. Maintaining control through blood and heritage, they moved in small circles. Behind every single war fought in Earth's grim history, *'The Priesthood's'* game became—*'separate to generate'*: totalling incredible power. Creating pseudo-realities became their primary objective for humans: worlds indistinguishable from computer realities—inauthentic ones.

Seeking to remove people out of their natural biorhythm, *'The Priesthood,'* altered time. Ancient Egyptians used sundials and water clocks to measure time. The movement and position of the sun and moon had direct effects on all objects on Earth: if you could manipulate time, you could manipulate human behaviour. Many emperors throughout time, changed the calendar—they played with it.

The first Roman calendar (738 BCE) consisted of 10 months and a year of 304 days. 10 months were named: *Martius, Aptilis, Maius, Janius, Quintilis, Sextilis, September, October, November, and December*. The last six names deriving from words for numbers—five, six, seven, eight, nine, and ten. In 452 BCE Emperor Numa added the month of January to the beginning of the year, and February to the end—corresponding to the solar year. Numa created a new month called: *Mercedinus,* consisting of 23 or 24 days, placing it between February 23rd and 24th—every other year. Manipulation of the calendar caused autumn to appear in July and winter in September. In 46 BCE, at invitation by Julius Caesar, Cleopatra visited Rome: her astronomers conversed with the Roman astronomer *Sosigenes*—making recommendations to improve the calender.

The new calendar consisted of 365 and 1/4 days. Twelve months contained 30 and 31 days, except February—possessing 29 days and 30 days—every four years. The beginning of the New Year also moved, from March 1st to January 1st. Honouring the new Julian calendar, Romans renamed the month of *Quintilis* (July)—after Roman Emperor Julius Caesar—calling it July, the month of his birth. Dying in 44 BCE, Augustus replaced Caesar. Month *Sextilis* (August) became newly named after Emperor Augustus. Scared of being overshadowed by Caesar, Augustus added an extra day to August—making his month as long as Caesar's. July and August became the only consecutive months with—31 days.

February was reduced to 28 days, with an additional day added every four years. The Julian calendar remained for more than 1500 years, until Pope Gregory XIII introduced the *'Gregorian calendar.'* Time became based on the birth of Jesus BC/AD. The Gregorian calendar was a farce. Latin *'decem,'* translated into the number ten:

"So why was December the 12th month?"

'The Priesthood' had nothing to worry about: nobody would question these strange—*spells.*

Removing women from their divine cycle: *'The Priesthood'* removed the 13th month. Thirteen months of twenty eight days, was the original cycle. The woman's menstrual cycle naturally tuned into the Moon. Altering this, they kept women in an hourglass—lost in time. The information was buried deep within *'The Circle of Trust'*— preserved over centuries. Tronan's ancestry could be traced back to the ancient priesthood; however, his grip of control loosened daily; it was slowly becoming—undone. We had to confront Tronan, to stop him; a master plan was—essential.

THE WALK

Luz wore no make-up and still dazzled my eyes as we took a beach stroll to calm our senses. Luz suffered turbulent bouts of depression and walking alleviated her ailments.

"Why does evil exist?" Luz sighed.

"Because of free will; we have the gift of choice. Good and evil serve the womb of the planet, they help restore balance," I replied.

The air became cooler, as we walked further into the night. We stopped to face each other—our irises locked. I pierced into her deep set eyes: like I was seeing Luz, for the first time. Our foreheads touched and I felt the hot gushing blood rush throughout her body. Quiet silent waves, crashed against our bodies—in this moment, we become one. Our arms came together in a powerful embrace, this is what we—needed.

Furious flames arose within, making my heart burn for her. I tasted her warm lips; a pleasant sweet nectar. Luz's cool waters passed over me, drenching my wild bush fires: tasting her ecstasy; closing eyes—seeing more clearly. She transported me to another plane, another time zone. Pulses synchronised to the same rhythms, as our tongues danced in unison. Our saliva became one; as we swam together. Drowning inside her waters on purpose, I became unconscious—like a sailor lost at sea—refusing to be rescued.

Feeling her breath on my neck; I listened to the smooth wind, the sways of her breath; I heard the harmonious orchestras play out. Composing music while birthing sound: only made our connection stronger. Swimming up to shore, inhaling smooth breaths of air—her presence tranquilised my soul. Leaning forward, I pressed my forehead against hers as our tongues became paralysed in the marvellous silence. Speaking no words—communicating through primal sounds—we entered our primal state—the most natural one.

Shaking sand from her flip flops: I stared in awesome wonder. The moment ended in a flash of light, but we knew this was just the beginning. We had sown the seeds. Heading back to our 'Earthship'—satisfied smiles shone from—beneath our faces.

Proteus's stained teeth protruded as he yelled at Pandora, arguing who had finished the toilet roll. Proteus blamed her as they both refused to accept responsibility. Despite these temporary hiccups, they got along well. Proteus moved his hand in front of Pandora's face—realising the insignificance of their petty dispute—wisdom kicked in. They began laughing:

"You are so wrong," said Proteus, imitating Pandora's North West London accent.

Rocking back and forth on her hammock, Pandora cooled down: her dark chocolate eyes—fixating on Proteus's fingers as he spread them across his rosewood. Burning Tibetan incense from the background added to the ambience. Still holding hands—Luz and I joined them outside. Smiling, Pandora and Proteus clapped in accord, bellowing:

"Hurray!"

"Let's celebrate, get out the glasses."

"You did not go there, did you? We knew it," said Pandora, giggling underneath her fragile lips.

Cracking ribs, Proteus ran to give me a painful bear hug—while Pandora kissed Luz on the cheeks: they shared our joy. A powerful excitement invaded the air: the four of us were family. Finding each other in times of crisis when London was ablaze: a crumbling battlefield. Birds of the same feather flock together—we were drawn to each other, like *'Neo-*

dymium' magnets—kindred spirits. In the presence of the right company, miracles happen: I found this to be—true. The secret I stumbled across, showed me what we gave out, we attracted to us. I realised when like minds connected—everything shifted.

Raising her head, Pandora glanced into the night, counting stars. Luz gazed up to see if *Tryathon* revealed itself—to see if the star still shone for us.

Luz's kiss unblocked my energy meridians, however, stuffy heat from the burning incense blocked them again.

"Let's go to *Merry Maidens*," I said, removing my shirt in desperate frustration. Three exasperated voices responded:

"Please, let's go!"

Proteus wiped the sweat from his forehead, as a cold breeze chilled our bodies. I became fond of the *'Iron Age'* relics: the nineteen-stone *Merry Maidens* ancient circles inspired souls—lifting them.

Dropping to his knees, Proteus began panting hard as we proceeded along the arduous trek. He had given up cigarettes a long time ago—but they still haunted him. Upon reaching, Pandora closed her eyes, twirling arms in 360 rotations. Kneeling down, Luz pressed her scorching cheeks on the side of the rocks—inhaling. Forming a full circle—we clenched hands together, closing eyes in tight grips. Humming and chanting—facing heads up towards the naked sky—glaring down on us.

Giant waves of energy engulfed us—infusing with possessed bodies. Squinting, Proteus observed the sky open its legs as energies poured forth the—ethereal ethers.

Numbers began entering our minds without consent—swirling, twirling, spiralling out of control. Plethoras of colours emerged as grounds beneath bellowed to disturb silence. Colourful exotic paints filling blank canvasses in our minds—adorned them with grace.

"Numbers upon numbers"— the last thing we saw, before collapsing into oblivion.

Slumbering into a deep sleep – an exquisite remoteness, our bodies lay arrested on the ground. Solving equations, our minds cracked the codes. Absent from this 3D reality—we opened the *portals*—us.

We became—'Number Makers'—'*Daring to Dream.*'

THE BELLY OF THE BEAST

SYLVANNUS'S JOURNAL - 2049 APRIL 9TH

I live in the belly of the beast.

I can see it survives by eating us.

I see how it distracts us.

How it uses magic to show us something that is not there.

The greatest deception we ever had was wearing clothes.

We are still not ready to be—naked.

CHAPTER NINE

MASTERMIND

PANDORA started devising a plan. A born scribe: a word manipulator and yesterday she became a number one. The four of us dived daily into pure crystal salt water – neutralising bodies becoming paramount to our Earth existence. A long winding road lied ahead of us– a shaky journey: skills would be tried. This would be a grand undertaking, a dangerous engagement indeed. We never viewed ourselves as martyrs—we lived with nothing to die for but everything to live for. Neither humanity's saviours, nor their superiors: we were only responding to – our calling. 'New London' taught us you had to grab life by the horns, you might not get another—chance.

Everything in 'New London' became controlled through the central machine: a machine called: *'Medea.'* This cunning machine created confusion and distraction beyond belief. Separating us from authentic reality: it sought to turn us into sluggards. *'Medea'* acted as the medium, a gateway: the gap standing between us was the barrier which we needed to go through, to find—the truth.

We knew disabling this grotesque machine would be the city's solution: stopping Tronan's propaganda machine was crucial—we had to shut it down:

"But how do you stop a train, generating more speed every year, for the last few thousand? Have do you stop a machine on autopilot?"

These questions perplexed us: it was imperative we seek a solution—fast.

HACKING BLOTIX

"We need to hack inside the mind of Blotix," said Proteus.

Expert skills to perform the complicated procedure lied within him: it required great patience, if the hack was to be successful. Blotix acted as the world's encyclopaedia, Earth's web. The world spied on itself in 2049 AD. Live web cams hung on every street in the world. Sun dwellers topping up tans in tropical beaches like *'Ipanema'* (Rio de Janeiro), could be watched in live time—Blotix monitored Earth—turtle island.

Governed and controlled by Tronan, it offered him a power like none other. Many believed, Blotix sprang from nowhere labelling it: *rudderless*: however, Tronan knew its true origins: he helped bring it into—fruition. Censorship on Blotix became a big issue in 2049 AD, increasing since 2020 AD. World leaders – afraid their populous were waking up in swarms, chose to ban certain websites. Information flooded the world: we lived in the digital age: it was inevitable some sought to—stop it.

The news feed on Blotix displayed current events around the world. Governed by Tronan's spin doctors: they had the last word of what appeared on Blotix. True masters of deception—this is what they lived for, what turned them on. Specialising in insincerity—this was the only food, which satisfied their greedy appetites. They thrived off fear produced by the masses. This is what kept them in power, what held them together: this was their glue—their binding.

By disabling Blotix, we could loosen Tronan's grip, his control over billions. We were certain we could make Tronan feel nervous:

"So why not give him something—to think about?"

The next step in Pandora's mastermind was for us to cross realms. Tryathon possessed technology, we could utilise: technologies superseding Earth's by light years. We needed to bring the city to a standstill—a crunching pause. We wanted the city to fall to its knees—hear its voice, its annoying—echo. Tronan of late was gathering loyal supporters throughout the city. He wooed crowds: those benefiting from his authoritarian dictatorship. At any one time, Tronan walked with up to ten bodyguards—it was in his nature. To get near him—impossible! You would be risking your life. Many even spoke of him having body doubles—identical clones. Apparently all the elite did, it was mandatory—standard.

Tronan walked with invisible spheres surrounding his body. This new technology designed for him could resist any type of assault, any type of laser beam—the ultimate as far as protection went. Our plan was to locate Tronan's movements, his hiding places. We aimed to monitor his steps: just as he—monitored ours.

Pandora continued to scribe as we spoke, even when we did not. The four of us knew we were walking on thin ice, on fragility. We had to watch our steps—steady feet would be required. Proteus kept scratching the top of his head, as he attempted to hack inside of 'Blotix.' His bloodshot red eyes became more apparent after passing the eleven hour mark. His overstretched retinas made him see double, turning him into a prime candidate for developing—'Myopia.'

Myopia was an eye disease, which was the top leading cause of vision loss throughout the world in 2049: it was a type of refractive error of the eye. Staring at screens being one of the many contributory factors, for birthing the disease. Eyes fixated on computers for prolonged periods acted as catalysts to help trigger the disease into motion.

Nobody ever attempted something on this scale since 'Dr. Pingo's' days – however, this would be remembered: its sting—lasting forever. The plan we agreed:

Luz, Pandora and I would cross realms into Tryathon, while Proteus commenced with hacking.

Following directions to *'Pendersick Castle,'* I spotted Gothlin's absence upon arriving. His predictions proved true: we no longer needed him. Gothlin's disappearance made us reflect on his inspiring spirit—you don't know what you got—'til its gone.

'Number Makers' required unique gestures to cross realms. Gothlin's gesture began, waving his sceptre, before piercing it to the ground. We practiced exit gestures—like we were on stage at the 'Apollo'—like audiences paid good money.

Upon entering the portal, Luz swung hair back and forth, while Pandora rolled her neck in divine synchronicity. Jumping to the castle ceiling before crashing to the ground—I felt my ribs squeeze—no pain, no gain.

Ferocious winds developed, as ice waters flooded the castle. Pandora's feet dangled in limbo as numbers entered our minds. Mass ripples of light swept across the ground, piercing crystal waters beneath. Struggling to open eyes in the freezing water, Luz noticed powerful vortex formations—showcasing talents. Our bodies shook back and forth—like circus animals being bullied to perform. Pandora's knackered arms wrestled to stay afloat as the ocean became darker. Spewing out infinite waters—peering at Tryathon's vast surface, I breathed in relief: Tryathon's doors opening—once again.

THE CRYSTALS

Foreseeing our coming, Hathora hovered over the waters, greeting us. Knowing we possessed abilities to unlock codes, a greater trust developed.

"Come with me," Hathora said, flashing rays of elaborate lights.

Full of enthusiasm, the three of us followed—our minds now opened. Making spiral shapes, Pandora imitated the gorgeous *streams of light*—they were everywhere.

Hovering around, I freed my soul, before Hathora brought us to an exquisite opening in the ground:

"Down here, this is where we harvest the technology," Hathora whispered. Floating down, we saw something—we'll never forget:

'Crystals upon crystals, submerged in deep waters.'

Broad waters stretched into the dark—marking territories. Reflections from the crystals alone were enough to blind anyone. Staring into the crystals; we marvelled at their intricate architecture. Resembling many precious stones found in Earth: diamonds, rubies, sapphires—we never had to work again.

"This is the technology you need, to disable Tronan's forces. These crystals are powerful beyond measure; they are being born as we speak," said Hathora, stunning turquoise lights at us. Luz reached out to touch one of the stones, before vanishing into a black hole.

"She will be back," said Hathora, "fear not."

"What is the purpose of these crystals?" I asked.

"To restore balance, to harmonise us," Hathora replied in calm grace.

Luz returned to us in a flash, tempted to touch the crystals—I resisted.

Tryathon's scenery was astronomic, colossal. We followed Hathora further into the unknown. Tryathon appeared to be a miner's paradise; a classic fairy tale—the serene ambience enthralled us all.

Turning to face us, Hathora spoke:

"This is why those who rule over you, place such a high bounty on these precious stones. These crystals and diamonds became treasured—idolized. They hold an immense power; it is this reason they guard these stones.

"In every one of your technologies, there is a crystal at the heart. Computer chips on Earth comprise of *crystalline silicon*. The crystals indigenous to Tryathon are called: '*Memners*'—working only in the hand of a 'Number Maker.' Take these crystals and commune with them—they will tell you what to do.

"Carry them into your cities, your streets: shine them on your people. Flash them in the eyes of those who rule over you, blind them with the lights. This battle will not be easy, but it must be fought. Order must be restored to Earth—she has bathed in the fires of hell—long enough," said Hathora.

Holding the crystals, we hurried to the blue gold ocean. Submerging heads underneath: we buried our ethereal bodies into its coolness. Hathora encouraged us to surrender whilst crossing—to let go. The second time crossing made Luz more confident—she knew the drill. The routine became programmed into cells: the process—etched in our minds. We swam down, until spiralling into the murky abyss. Numbers swarmed into our minds, as we surrendered to the infinite waters. In a flash of light: the *'Atlantic Ocean'* welcomed us—we came back down to—Earth.

It took only a flicker, before Luz began riding the waves of *'Praa Sands'*: clenching the *Memners* in her soaking hands—they illuminated the—dark starry night. The *Memners* light could not be concealed—they refused to.

We found Proteus in the exact position we left him: his eyes still glaring at the holographic computer: nothing changed—only we did.

DECODING THE MACHINE: BEHIND THE WIZARD'S CURTAIN

The breakthrough, coming at the 32nd hour, forced Proteus to relax his mutilated shoulders. Managing to hack inside 'Blotix,'— he needed a cigarette – smoke needed to be blown. His eyes folded in on themselves: he became an exhausted zombie. Against all odds – doing the impossible – opening a can of worms in Tronan's face. The three of us gathered around the computer, as he began to 'daisy chain.' This was a hacking technique where you gained entry to a computer and used it to gain access to another. Hackers who got away with database theft did this and then backtracked, meaning, they went backward after doing what they intended and covered their tracks—by destroying logs.

We called Proteus 'The Wizard,' because he possessed the detailed knowledge of how to hack. Orphaned as a child: his uncle raised him—providing the best he could. Despite an unstable upbringing, he never let his childhood stunt his growth: it never interfered with his—love for computers.

He knew a computer's mind, its vulnerabilities: understanding how complex pieces of software and hardware worked inside of the computer. Many of the hacking techniques Proteus used were stepped in *deep magic*. This was a code based on esoteric knowledge. The deep magic Proteus applied, lacked any theoretical explanation: it was an advanced technique, saturated in obscurity—pure wizardry.

Inspired by writings of Arthur C. Clarke (the author of *'2001, A Space Odyssey'*): Proteus remembered the words of Arthur daily: his favourite quote, becoming his mantra:

"Any sufficiently advanced technology is indistinguishable from magic."

Proteus could hack anything: a car, a train, an airport—whatever we wanted. He could bring us closer to our mission. Studying the art of *cryptography* since eleven—mastering applications, he viewed life as a walk in the park. *Cryptography* was the science of hiding information: similar to *Steganography*—the art of hiding messages in plain sight. Using both to seduce Blotix—additional *'masquerading'* techniques—put the final nail in the coffin. These were attacks where somebody forged their identity, by supplying false credentials when hijacking existing connections through—*man in the middle attacks*.

Proteus had to write a *'script,'* paralysing 'Blotix's' safeguards. He had to enter 'Blotix's' spine—uprooting it—tearing it apart. Thirteen major root servers inside Blotix connected the world together—the world was smaller than we thought. Shutting down 'Blotix,' however, would be temporary—it would soon be living its—life after death.

'Blotix' was unimaginably huge, laced with intricacy. If a server went down: they could just route your traffic around it, until it revived itself. However, Proteus's paralysis to the system would still give Tronan chills—make him wrap up more appropriately. Getting rid of Blotix would require a year of Proteus's magic—we never had that time.

Blotix, an invertebrate, lacked a backbone. A network of networks: it acted as a holographic internet world. Think of it as a rhizome: a mass of roots at the bottom of a tree: acting like entities, whose connection to each other was—*conceptually indeterministic*: meaning—there was always another way in—always.

Against time: the countdown started as soon as the virus duplicated itself. From this moment onwards, our coordinates would be located—tracked down.

Gathering, 'Earthship' essentials, we prepared to head into the city. Tronan's forces would be knocking, armed with lasers—time was of the essence. Sprinting to the kitchen, Proteus left the holographic computer on the table—he had a wicked sense of humour. Dashing for the door, we grabbed our bulging rucksacks, filled with supplies we required—fruits—lots of them. Luz's fingers squeezed in 'Granny Smith' apples—stuffing our rucksacks with food galore. Requiring sustenance, a long journey awaited us: travelling into the city would be arduous. Leaving all electronic equipment at home became imperative, we needed to remain—untraceable.

'The crystals!' Luz yelled.

We grabbed them, while jetting for the door. We walked out to the main road nearest our residence.

"NEW LONDON," Pandora's sign read in clear bold black.

Waiting there, Pandora focused on her red finger nails—killing time. Poking her head forward, Luz spotted a white lorry as Proteus jumped in the air—waving hands. Hitching a ride in the back—we were off. The lorry driver transporting salmon fish into 'New London's' heart—seemed recognisable. Proteus pinched his nose as we sat covered in fish—dead fish.

Apart from putrid smells of decomposing matter, we were fine—just relieved to be in transit. Movement was the primary concern at this point—everything else came second. The *'X-matron'* became the standard method of transportation in the city. Neither of us possessed one; it wasn't necessary. Ironically however, if we did have the *'X-matron,'* we would have arrived in 'New London' in three quarters of the time—never mind.

WATER IS THE ESSENCE

SYLVANNUS'S JOURNAL - JUNE 5TH 2049

I etch my name in the sand, but the moment I write – not soon after, the ocean washes it away.

What's the meaning?

Water is the essence.

Water takes the impression of everything around us.

The ultimate conundrum—how can the water ever understand itself?

That would be like fire trying to understand what it felt like to be hot, or like water trying to understand what it felt like to be wet.

The infinite waters can never be contained, only dived into.

Everything is unique.

Nature would never create two of the same: that would be boring.

Moulding matter begins with our words: they are the incantations—*spells*.

CHAPTER TEN

MAYHEM—THE CITY'S NIGHTMARE

LASER shots fired down our Earthship doors, leaving them smouldered. Arriving inside, Tronan's forces ransacked the place—crucifying it. Rebels cordoned off 'Praa Sands' and surrounding areas for further investigation. Tronan's forces took everything of value—paintings, jewellery, silverware and several thousand pounds in money. Deploying a two hundred man team to scan the *'Outskirts'*—local residents were questioned regarding our whereabouts, interviews already underway. Sitting back in his plush 'Mayfair' suite: Tronan reached into the depths of his pockets, pulling out three dice. Moving them in a circular motion in his palms: he crunched his hands, before casting them to the ground.

"This is impossible!"

Howling to the top of his lungs, Tronan slammed down the top of his marble table.

"Tryathon!" he screamed, before lifting defeated hands to the air.

Grimacing, he turned to his closet associate Rosney:

"Who are these people?" screeched Tronan, gritting stained teeth.

"They remain undetectable, Sir," said Rosney, hesitating.

Tronan remained anaesthetised upon hearing Rosney's bleak response. Creases on his forehead heightened with his brewing fury. Crunching hands—he contracted them as tight as he could, until fists resembled miniature stress balls.

Growling, he murmured under his lips, mumbling inaudible sounds. His voice lacked clarity: his own voice began irritating him. Beating on his chest, his associates became concerned for his abnormal behaviour: he seemed confused—lost in ruins.

Gathering composure, Tronan raised his head as his wife Nephli approached. Providing hope, Nephli became his beacon of reassurance in times of crisis. Acting as his reinforcer and anchor—he was lost without her. Tronan buried his head in Nephli's bosom, rumpling his £50,000 vicuna suit. Vicuna, the world's most expensive fabric was softer, lighter and warmer than any other wool on Earth. Vicuna wool was also the finest fibre, capable of being spun at eight times finer than human hair. Tronan's suits reminded him of his importance of keeping a smile on his face in times of doubt.

Nephli ran her fingers through the back of Tronan's dark black hair—caressing him. Nephli's presence lowered his blood pressure, saved him from heart attacks. Glimpsing into his eyes, Nephli began whispering in his ear: Tronan laughed as the atmosphere lightened. They possessed a deep chemistry: she helped him make better decisions. Placing hands on Tronan's forehead—he sat in his high chair, regaining focus. His murmuring ceased, until it faded into—blank silence.

'New London' was burning to pieces. The temporal shut down of 'Blotix,' serving as the catalyst, was enough to bring back memories of revolution—enough to remind people to demand change, no matter what cost. Burning flames from riots could be seen throughout the city. The tremendous heat reminded one what it felt like to live in deserts with no water. Rioting justified more control: however, it still made Tronan—uncomfortable.

Feeling an awkward dryness in his throat, Tronan coughed—imagining city smoke filling linings of his trachea—suffocating him. Ordering a fresh glass of mineral water, he proceeded out of his chair and gave orders. His forces were to check all vehicles heading from the *M5 Junction* into 'New London.'

Travelling into 'New London' made Pandora and Proteus fall asleep. Half the duration of the journey was spent in the inner depths of their minds. Keeping eyes wide open—Luz and I worked as unpaid watchmen. Pandora's eyelids laid in rest, enjoying the smooth ride: smooth enough to conserve our energy and take our minds elsewhere—to surrender.

The lorry jolted as 'New London' welcomed us.

"What a racket," moaned Luz, covering ears.

Moving hands to my chest, I felt the tension surge throughout my body—banging on bones. Pressure built and the anticipation grew thicker—rising like wild tsunamis. Blocked roads made it difficult to meander through the overpopulated city. We never made it into the heart—walking would be necessary to reach its chambers. Coming as far as we could go, we congratulated ourselves. Applying a subtle break, the lorry driver brought the vehicle to a grinding halt.

"Passes!" bellowed one of Tronan's forces.

Their voices became familiar through 'Blotix,' their sound—unmistakable. All of Tronan's forces used *Z voice modifiers*: altering voices so they were identical. Their mission became to threaten anyone who resisted their authority, to intimidate them. *Z voice modifiers* served the purpose, to make voices more recognisable—allowing authority to be understood for those with hearing loss.

"Get out of the vehicle Sir, we need to search the vehicle," said a grubby overweight officer.

The lorry driver flashed his ID card, bearing a hard copy of his driving license. Leaving Tronan's forces wandering, authorities could not detect if it was authentic or fake. First glances became deceptive in 2049 AD—Earth had changed. His driving license could have been a counterfeit for all they knew. Hoards of individuals faked ID's, attempting to cross the city. Authorities needed to scan his iris—check his real identity.

"Get out of the vehicle!" yelled another officer.

Tones from their voices picking up speed, displayed their true intentions.

Trembling from the panic, Proteus's hands shook, hitting Luz by accident. Pandora also woke up—disturbing commotions bringing us all out of *'La La Land.'* Sitting in a state of heightened awareness, we sat as still as a rock in a hard place—hearing the wind—breathe.

Recognising the driver before hitching the ride, we attempted to remember his face. Appearing in *'The Outskirts,'* he passed along the main road near us every now and then. We knew him from a glance—trusting him, we believed he was on our side.

"I will not get out of this vehicle!' insisted the driver. "I know my rights, I know the law."

Laughing in his face, officers grabbed him by the collar. His arms jerked upwards as they yanked him out of the vehicle—like a dusty rug. Throwing him onto hard concrete: the driver laid on the ground, curled up like a worm, waiting to be preyed upon.

Pandora eardrums caught the brunt of the thunderous banging on the vehicle's side. Our heads shook, juddering back and forth like the machine filled city.

"In the split second life flashes before your eyes, what do you do? What can you do?"

Carrying neither plan A or B—there was no dress rehearsal, this was it. We stared at each other in blank silence, our chances appearing slim.

"It's only fish in here Sir, only fish, dead fish," said an officer, opening the back door of the lorry.

Breaths warmed lips from sighs of relief: blood pressure began to lower, bringing calm.

"Empty everything out, clear the whole lot. Our orders were to check everything—everything!" roared a scrawny senior officer.

Thinking fast would save us—improvisation became crucial.

Bucket loads of fish poured outside the vehicle in droves. Tronan's forces trampled salmon heads as they found their way inside the vehicle. Equipped with technology of the most powerful kind, they viewed this as an easy chore. They received the best Tronan could offer them. The officers carried infra-red scanning devices, which checked vehicles without even stepping foot inside. However, orders were for manual checks: everything was to be done by—humans.

Hundreds of dead fish spread scaly fins onto streets—they were all over the place. Aromas filling our nostrils forced us to smell their foul odour.

"I can see something, Sir!" grunted an officer.

The officers took out thermal measuring devices: they located us in seconds. An eerie silence permeated the atmosphere. We remained as still as possible, given our cramped circumstances. Luz stared at Tronan's forces right in their eyes. Eye to eye: we were now seated at adjacent ends of them. Jagged yellow teeth revealed themselves as smiles on their faces grew larger. They smiled at their discovery, at their jewels—us.

Laser beams dotted Pandora's beige cardigan. The officers caressed their triggers—toying with ideas of whether or not to pull them. Our fate lay in their hands: our presence made their mission simpler. We prayed—prayed as we had never done before—that we would be safe. Proteus chewed on his lips, until they bled. We knew time turned against us: it would not be long before guts were blown to smithereens. Our blood would be used to repaint city walls—to restore them.

A great paradox occurring within, made me describe the experience—'*intellectually incomprehensible.*' During the fearful moment, a deep calm pierced my body: time slowed, and I began seeing numbers upon numbers. Shooting officers smirking glances—numbers flooded my mind. A stunned Luz watched my head rocket back and forth, giving off appearances of wild convulsions. Perplexed, officers squeezed triggers, gritting teeth with—no mercy.

Eardrums burst from whining screams of lasers. Officers held lasers in tight clutches, continuing ruthless onslaughts of abrupt fires. Beams lingered in the air surrounding us.

"Were we shot? What the hell was happening?"

Turning battered heads to face irate officers—they were still hammering. We only heard sounds—violent squeals of fierce lasers. Heavy drops of water crashed upon the roof—fracturing its surface. The vehicle brimmed over with water. Pandora saw the *Memners* submerged from the corner of her eye – we could feel their power. An intense energy arose within our bodies, from the base of our spines.

In the spur of the moment, a rapid heat grew inside the lorry. Luz held her bleeding stomach, as our clothes incinerated into thin ash. Covering ears, officers ducked as windows smashed, shattering chunks of thick glass —carving tattoos on their faces. Luz struggled, as water proceeded to bury her nostrils. Suspended in air, stretching stiff fingers—the lorry exploded into thick plumes of smoke.

The Four of us stood where the vehicle once was. Everything was gone, nothing was left—only us.

THE LIGHT WARS

SYLVANNUS'S JOURNAL - MARCH 3RD 2049

The light wars began a long time ago on Earth.

We were told we came from the same origins? We were misguided.

What do we know about our Earth? What were we told?

How much of it is true?

Some people were born to keep this system going, some were born to tear it apart.

I would like to consider myself in the category of the latter.

This cannot go on any longer: not because I say so, but because we all know—we are stuck.

Why do we tell lies to our children? Why do we suffocate them?

Have you not seen enough suffering? Have you not seen your fate?

I see you running: I hear your heart pound.

Rocking back and forth on your chair, questioning why?

I see your face, when others are not looking: I see what they cannot.

The oceans run deep, so why do we stay on the surface?

What are we afraid of? How long will it take before we open our eyes?

How long will it take before we touch the truth with our bare hands?

I see your fury—we are all furious.

We burn fires and use our bodies as the charcoal.

There is no path, therefore I do not follow the straight road—I follow my own.

Do not follow me, for I will only you lead you astray; I will only lead you to the wolves.

Look at yourself.

Look at the worms that crawl inside you.

Even the animals are afraid of you; you've have made everything your enemy.

The hole in your heart is obvious—it's transparent.

I see right through you.

I see your pretentious nature; I see you judge before you think.

How much longer are you willing to hold onto the cliff top, without calling for help?

How much longer, are you willing to stay there?

I see your denial, your refusal to accept defeat.

I observe your restless nature.

Why has your inner voice been muted out?

What terrors are contained within them?

Away from home: the castaway—abandoned.

Lost in your own darkness.

Who taught you how to serve? How to accept without question?

Who made you into the perfect slave?

Who was the author?

THE LIGHT WARS

CHAPTER ELEVEN (11:11:11)

"WHAT'S A LIFE WORTH?"

LUZ'S arms remained airborne: her eyes faced my back and her hair became vertical. Diaphragms digging into collar bones made dying pulses audible as she lay unconscious over my abused shoulders. Bloodstains beryl red camouflaged with my red jacket made it difficult to distinguish. Trawling through the beaten city, I covered her mouth—avoiding cigarette smoke. Her hollow shell jolted as I strode up worn pavements—a far cry from what she once was. Pandora's eyes blurred, focusing to track the three of us. Waving his hands, Proteus attempted to clear the dust filled atmosphere.

We wandered through the city like prisoners of war—limping like the city owed us. Debris of burnt flags littered the ground. Dissembled billboards and city rubbish turned Proteus's black boots a dishevelled grey. Our shoes dragged through what laid beneath us—the little left.

Squealing sirens alarmed us of the re-emergence of Tronan's rebels. Glimmering lights adorned the city's face: lights from cigarettes, lights from the lasers—lights from souls who hid themselves for so long. Moving Luz's weightless arm to the side, I peered into the distance. Glancing as far as eyes would carry us, until the roads end—we saw only—destruction.

Crowd roars echoed against city walls, creating acoustics. Crowd clamours could not be ignored, nor would they be. Seas of voices from mass demonstrations in 'Hyde Park' and 'Edgware road,' filled the ethers. North, West, East, South London became a zoo. Laying Luz's thrashed body on 'Trafalgar square's' grounds—tears rained, touching her cheeks. Panicking I knelt, blowing hordes of air into her mouth—she never responded. My heart's blood became thick — refusing to move, refusing to leave Luz. She was my treasure—a brilliant reason to live.

"What's a life worth?" I screamed, until Proteus and Pandora restrained me.

Clasping my jacket, Proteus pinned me down – preventing me from headbanging the concrete. Paralysed from staring at Luz's lifeless body—I couldn't believe my eyes. She never entered the city to go down like this—she deserved more. Feeling guilty, her blood was on my hands, literally.

Surveying the sky, Pandora covered her face with both hands. Pulling tired eyelids down towards her cheeks – she held her pose, before collapsing to the ground. We were now in the heart of 'New London,' in the amphitheatre. Trapped in its cage – we heard the lions roar, the gladiators had – risen.

NEPHLI UNVEILED

Undressing in front of Tronan, Nephli placed her hands on her breasts.

"This is what the city has become: bare, empty, naked—it can finally see itself.

"Why did you let this city fall?

"Why did you cause our annihilation?

"We will fall with this city, we will perish.

"Our time is short—I have already seen it," whispered Nephli.

Extending hands, she placed them on Tronan's neck. Massaging his muscles, Nephli rolled her hands in circular motions. Firmer grips with each rotation made beautiful hands sore. Imitating to strangle him—moving clenched fingers inches away, she drew them closer in mimicking motions. Tronan's neck flinched backwards, avoiding further discomfort. Clasping both hands, he forced sharp fingernails into her palms—suspending them, before flinging them to the ground.

Putting his hands under Nephli's neck, he lifted her up, holding her in a brutal 'chokehold.' Pedicured feet levitated off his 'Mayfair' bedroom—disconnected from the ground. Tronan glanced at Nephli's beauty spots, before lowering her to the floor. Gasping for air, her neck swelled. Bowing her head—eyes faced the flooring, defenceless: her naked body laying there, camouflaged with the solid marble grounds beneath.

"So now the masses too must know?

"Why did you lay down your guard?

"Why did you succumb to their screams?

"Why did you let their nightmares wake you up?" Nephli said, frowning.

Becoming more passionate with each word—seeping waters trickling from corners of eyes, smudged brown topaz mascara everywhere. Biting fingernails—she began to gnaw on them.

Tilting her head up to Tronan, Nephli spoke:

"You fool!

"How could you betray us?

"How could you break the circle? Break *'The Circle of Trust'*—the circle you were entrusted in?" cried Nephli.

Piercing Tronan like rusty arrows, her words hit like daggers—unwashed. Resonating with him, Nephli's words rung true. A born clairvoyant, a natural seer: Nephli held the title of *'New London's'* city oracle.

"You have no faith. I pity your kind, your vermin. The words you speak produce acid rain. They cause my heart to ache, my body to burn. They make me feel weak, frail, disabled," said Tronan, raising his voice in pitch.

"Only you make yourself weak, you lack courage. You embarrass our ancestors, you disrespect them. You will burn—die a painful death," shrieked Nephli, squinting her eyes.

"Silence!" Tronan screamed.

His roar reverberated throughout his entire

mansion—shaking everything. Neck veins bulged, spreading outwards—protruding, as if his whole body had to support his statement, even if no one else would. Nephli's strained neck bowed, facing the ground. Swinging his foot, Tronan kicked her red sequoia dress over her face—blinding her. Banging the door behind him—leaving her there, he had better things to do. Nephli's body lay still—frozen like a statue.

"Do we know these people? Who are they?" screamed Tronan to Rosney.

"Number Makers Sir," replied Rosney, keeping his composure.

"They cracked the codes Sir, they travelled between worlds. They know of Tryathon. Our forces found them in the back of a lorry. A driver hid them, whilst transporting salmon into the city, Sir.

"They carried the *Memners*—Lord, we stood no chance," said Rosney, becoming emotional.

Cracking knuckles, Tronan's saliva became frothy in his mouth; holding it there, he refused to swallow. Tronan's pupils expanded, spilling over into his scleras. Rolling shoulders back, he unlocked them—freeing himself from chains cast. Staring at dots—rolling dice danced on his floor. He lit his 'Cuban,' contracting lips, as he blew back smoke. The wild aroma filled his mansion; it became his—breathing space.

After an interval of cold silence, he spoke:

"Kill them! Kill them all!

"We depend on these ants for our existence, but if we must perish, let them perish with us. Burn them all!

"Until only ashes remain," said Tronan.

A CITY IN CHAOS

Laser beams sprayed 'New London' like Sierra Leone mosquitoes. Walking in single file through the city made Proteus feel childish. Luz's neck rested over my back, her hair touched my knees. Mass crowds in *'Piccadilly Circus,'* made it difficult to see. Tronan's forces carried lasers, they had what the masses never. Technology made it possible for silent wars, however, this city made noise. Tronan's squad pushed further; the masses only had their voices and this was being drowned out. Seeing this as an opportunity to tame the masses—waging war against them, gave Tronan something to do. His rebels stormed through the city like drones—like mindless automatons, connected to machines—devoid of consciousness.

Riding around in foreign vehicles, unknown to us—rebels concealed themselves in powerful black machines, becoming their alter egos. Wearing thick black masks—unleashing poisonous smoke, they became the city's nemesis. Enthusiasm dimmed as we saw their assemblage, as the city became beleaguered. Laying Luz's bashed body on the pavement, I protected it. The three of us discussed the few options left; we began activating our 99%—dormant brain capacity.

Shutting down 'Blotix' by Proteus made authorities demure; however, this was short lived—ephemeral. The masses never had the wherewithal to defend themselves—forbearance toppled, crowds surrendering to their knees. Hair raised from our heads, as planes swooped over—firing down on us like ants being crushed by inattentive *passerbyers*. Tronan's' forces territory moved further into the city; we became small—tiny microscopic nothings.

"What were our chances against them?

"Where could we possibly go from here?

"What was going to be the city's panacea?"—We were all guessing.

LORD NEPTIS

Entering one of the many opulent rooms his mansion housed, Tronan walked towards a vault, located at the back. Inserting a code, he remembered the numbers by heart. Opening a small box, he knelt on one knee, placing hands on top. Containing patterns of hand imprints, the box carried his unique signature.

Tronan began praying, as eyes fixated on the gold box:

"Oh *'Governor of Neptis,'* it is I, Tronan, that speaks. I know you see us, that you see what befalls us. I ask for you to reveal yourself: I ask for you to show us that you are working with us—through us. Our prayer is that you acknowledge our presence, that you feel it. We have served you for aeons, now we ask you to return the favour: we ask for you to offer us your forces—your reinforcements. The planet has reawakened, Earth is coming back alive. Her rivers rage—she is remembering. Her elements move faster, they seek to be reunited: they torment us. We hear the screams of her children: we hear their—squalls.

"Darkness fills the streets: we battle with her. We will not give up the fight: so we ask you father, we the children of you—show us light—illuminate us once again.

"The gates of Tryathon have opened. Many from Earth have already travelled there: they know of the secrets. They walk with the *Memners*. The *Memners* walk amongst us, they have arisen. We feel their heat: their furious wrath has become—inescapable.

"Their light fills streets, exposing our treachery. *Lord,* for centuries you helped us enslave Earth, you have reaped its benefit. Predictions were foretold in the great book—it was written. The writings showed the cycle would end, that our days were—numbered.

"Oh *Lord,* you have imbued in us, your children—your essence. We learnt to become masters of destiny, that we must guide the helm of the ship.

Through you, we learnt about dominion, rulership — that *'the power'* can never be given, it must be taken. You taught us the secret laws of the universe, ancient principles which mould us together. You made us aware of scared sciences, which govern all existence.

"You have nurtured us.

"*Lord,* watch over us, as we watch over them.

"We have built alters in your name. The masses give you praise of thanksgiving—they offer you themselves for sacrifice. As your children, we have done as you desire. Now the time has come. The waters have been opened. We are not ready to hand over power; we are not ready to surrender.

"*Lord,* prolong our time to govern over man, grant us mercy. Send forth your ships, technologies—weapons of war. Help us defeat those who wish to challenge our authority.

"Cast down your hand, the hand which has been invisible for so long; reveal yourself—ride with us.

"Fill our spirits with the blood you drink from Earth's sacrifice. Help us *Lord;* one more time again, we ask you—help us be—victorious," prayed Tronan.

'WHAT LIES BENEATH US?'

Pandora moved through the decomposing bodies lying beneath us. Rats began to feed on them and they enjoyed themselves. The city became a silhouette, a shadow of its former self. Water poured out through burst water pipes; the city became an ocean. Our weightless bodies advanced onto pavements which once were. Raising his head, Proteus looked up, flabbergasted:

"What the hell!"

Waves of ships focused down on us, their presence bringing a gripping silence. The city was brought to a standstill—its pulse stopped. Luz's ears became bullied from vivacious sounds emerging from the giant ships: they dwarfed us—we became deafened. Firing down powerful light rays—Tronan's prayers were answered, his voice heard.

Hiding in city cracks and crevices, Pandora followed contours as guides. Struggling to focus as lines blurred, Luz's body was taking its toll. Hovering in stationary positions, ships towered over the city like powerful dictators, like governors implementing corrupt laws. Spewing thick bands of light, they left craters in the ground—souvenirs. Pausing intermittently, the ships stopped only to witness their—carnage.

LOVE & WAR

Facing his bathroom mirror, Tronan's comb pierced his scalp as he dragged through his sparkling black hair. Grabbing a razor, he rolled up his sleeves and began scrapping his jaws. Black blood poured forth, staining his white sink. Exiting the bathroom, he proceeded to the kitchen. Opening the fridge, he poured a glass of cow's blood: this is what he lived off—what he drank for sustenance.

Heading into his 'Mayfair' office, Rosney adjusted his tie while smoothing out his collar: appearances mattered. Despite what was happening throughout the city, Tronan shed no tears, only dirty grins. This was his dream, an opportunity to exercise power, to its maximum capabilities. Protecting his family became paramount: Tronan ordered for family members to enter ships hovering above. His family would be safe there, out of harm's reach.

Hurrying, he collected sacred documents—lost ancient scrolls. Great maps existed within them—blueprints, maps illustrating how to build civilisations. These scrolls stored within them, the quintessential 'Earth' guide of how to rule forever.

"I will not go with you, I will remain here," said a calm Nephli, approaching Tronan.

Shrugging, Tronan turned his back on her:

"Do as thou wilt, your fate is not in my hands."

Making vile dents on the floor—storming past, he never flinched back once.

They parted company then—forever.

PREPARING THE CRYSTALS

Preparing the *Memners,* Hathora marvelled as they glistened , submerged in deep waters.

"Rise, oh my children, rise!" Hathora said.

Levitating—closing eyes, the *Memners* suspended themselves in thin empty space—hovering, awaiting Hathora's voice. Fluttering over to the vast *'streams of light,'* Hathora flashed their attention. *'Streams of light'* encircled her—spiralling, forming dome like shapes around her core.

Hathora started speaking:

"Follow us to the portal, travel the journey with us: help resurrect her. *'The Governor of Neptis,'* has awakened its ships—they tower over her.

"Oh, you that move freely—free her, send forth your aid.

"Deliver her from the evil that wicked men do.

"The time has come for a new beginning—a new Earth"

Intensifying evolutions around her—*'Streams of light'* swirled, deciding answers. Communicating through radiant flashes emanating from crystal cores – they were sociable brings. Reading signals, Hathora smiled in relief—they agreed.

Swooning towards the portal, the *Memners* and Hathora hurried behind.

Tryathon had arisen.

SQUARES AND NO CIRCLES

SYLVANNUS'S JOURNAL - JUNE 9TH 2049

Why are the windows around me square and not circle, like my eyes?

Can we look at anything without judgement, why do our opinions always have to get in the way?

How can you explore infinity?

The life never stops.

There is only the constant movement, the inhalation and exhalation.

One must never rest on their laurels.

I learn everything from nature.

The wind never stops, no matter how much it moves.

The wind is flawless in its ambition to be continuously present, always in the now.

CHAPTER TWELVE

"NEW EARTH—THE REBIRTH"

RECLINING in the *'Governor of Neptis's'* ship, Tronan smiled down as 'New London' burned away. Giggling, he held arms out in reverence for the Governor. 500 feet ships towered over Earth—becoming city watchmen. Tronan knew he would have to return to 'New Earth,'this Earth would be destroyed: it was breathing its last—breath.

Tronan's Earth reign was perishing, just as landscapes beneath. Possessing no power, Tronan's currency diminished. Clapping hands, he applauded Earth's performance as she destroyed herself.

Tronan gave commands for the 'Governor' to take him home—business was finished. 'The Governor' was not in any of the *ships*: he was in *'Neptis'*—controlling them.

Patting Tronan's back, Rosney grinned:

"This planet deserves to die," said Rosney.

"We all do," laughed Tronan.

Lunging sweaty fingers into his pockets, Tronan pulled out his three dice. He saw life as a game—he was losing. Thrusting his three dice into his eyes, he squealed—like a captured whale. He heard the skies roar, as they cracked and crumbled over his ship. Giant dents formed in the sky, leaving impressions on the milk grey clouds. Nephli's prediction passed—Tronan knew it would. There was no escape. Tronan's blood pressure rose, as he downed glasses of spirits. With nowhere to run, he became—'New London's' prisoner.

Deeper dents formed in the sky as *'streams of light'* burst forth through clouds. The *Memners* and Hathora followed—the whole of Tryathon entering Earth.

The *Memners* dropped themselves into city streets like hail stones—creating ripples in the ocean flooded city. Shaking grounds from the sheer velocity of their fall alerted Earth of their presence. Leaving the crevice, four of us swam through the city, exasperated. Luz's closed eyes collected water as she rode on my back. We looked up at what the world had become: we watched its—metamorphoses.

Tronan's ships ceased firing—unable to, they were paralysed. Circling ships, *'streams of light'* spiralled around, emitting lights which blinded their glass.

Tronan's melting face dripped on his Vicuna suit: the heat cooked his skin, smouldering it into thin ash. Boiling blood, his internal organs erupted—cremating him alive. His skin disintegrated into fractals—fractals of—nothingness.

Staring, as charred ships rained down from skies—wild fires began consuming them. Scorched by the flaming light-filled skyline, they vanished into the hollow void—the unoccupied abyss.

Moving arms through diamond waters, Luz paddled on her own accord—hearing Proteus's screams in the distance:

"A miracle!"

Swimming behind, Pandora yelled in disbelief:

"Sister!"

Adrenaline surged through my body, as I reached to hold her knackered hands. Her eyes widened as I kissed her warm lips—she was alive.

Hathora stared down at the *Memners*. *'New Earth'* had formed, signalling a new future. Reaching into our rucksacks—pulling out the *Memners,* we threw them into diamond waters. They were no longer needed, for we had become them: a sea of—crystals.

SUPER CHILDREN

SYLVANNUS'S JOURNAL - DECEMBER 21ST 2049

11:11 AM

Those super children being born, you know they're not afraid of you.

They know you're lying because they see you do not live what you talk about.

They are ready to fly, so why do you encourage them to walk?

They are here to show you something.

Something you may not be ready to look at, because you have been in denial for too long.

Call it clairvoyance if you will, they know more than you can imagine.

I now see the whole of life is a myth.

If you do not create your own story, someone will create one for you.

So I have developed my own story: my own myth about what this world is.

I am the architect now: the architect of my own reality.

All we have are the stories and at the end, the story

never dies.

It is only the stories that live on.

We wander through the story: it's all we have—for what are we without it.

THE TIME HAS COME

The time has come.

I'm smiling, I don't know why I'm smiling but I'm smiling.

I'm happy, I don't know why I am happy but I'm happy,

I feel like the luckiest man alive.

Peace, fills my lungs like water fills an aquarium tank,

Full of fishes,

This is it, this is what I've been waiting for,

Finally the time has come and it was worth it.

PANDORA'S WORD ARCHITECTURE

Accent–(Late Middle English)–Latin *accentus*: meaning intonation, the base elements of the Latin are *ad*–'to' and *cantus* 'song,' a song, sung to music.' The sense 'intonation' arises from the notion of a musical rise and fall being added to speech.

Act–(Late Middle English) the noun act is Latin from *actus* 'event,' thing done.

Aeroplane–(Late 19th Century)–this formation is from the French aeroplane, from *aero*–'air' and Greek–*planos* 'wandering.'

Aphrodisiac–emanating from Aphrodite, the Greek goddess of love.

Asterisk–(Late Middle English)–emanates from Greek *asteriskos* 'small star,' from *aster* 'star'

Atmosphere–(mid 17th Century)–Modern Latin *atmos-phaera,* from Greek *atmos* 'vapour' and sphaira 'globe'

Autograph–(early 17th century)–Greek *autographon,* 'written with one's own hand.' The base elements are *autos* 'self' and *graphos* 'written.'

Boss–(early 19th Century) deriving from Dutch *baas*:

meaning 'master'

Camouflage—(First World War) adopted from the French *camoufler* 'to disguise,' which was originally thieves slang.

Castle—Latin *castrum*: meaning 'fortified place'

Degree—Vulgar Latin *degradus*, 'a step down'

Demon—(Middle English) from the Greek *daimon* 'deity, genius'

Enigma—(mid 16th Century) from Greek *ainigma* 'riddle'

Ether—(Greek) from Greek aither 'upper air'

Fallacy—(late 15th Century) from Latin *fallere* 'to deceive'

Guilt—(Old English) the origin of Old English *gylt* 'failure of duty'

Humour—(Middle English) Latin *humor* 'moisture,' referring to 'bodily fluid,' hence to humour someone 'to indulge a person's whim.

Introvert—(mid 17th Century) Latin *introvertere*, from intro— 'to the inside' and *vertere* ' to turn,' 'to turn one's thoughts inwards (in spiritual contemplation)

Gypsy–(mid 16th century) Originally *gipcyan*, short for Egyptian: gypsies were popularly supposed to have come from Egypt.

Horoscope–(Old English) from Greek *horoskopos*, from *hora* 'time' and *skopos* 'observer'

Hospital–Latin *hospes*, 'guest, host,' the word hospital arrived in English around the turn of the fourteenth century, it denoted 'lodging for pilgrims and travellers'

Imagine–Latin *imaginare* 'form an image of, represent'

Intuition–Latin *intueri*, 'consider or contemplate'

Journey–(Late Middle English) from Old French *jornee* 'a day, a day's travel, a day's work'

Kaleidoscope–(early 19th century) Greek *kalos* 'beau-tiful,' *eidos* 'form,' and the suffix–scope (from Greek *skopein* 'look at')

Library–(Old English) Latin *Librarium*, 'a place to store books'

Labyrinth(Late Middle English)–referring to the mytho-logical maze constructed by the Greek craftsman Dae-dalus for King Minos of Crete to house the Minotaur, a creature half man half bull, from Greek *laburinthos*

Logic–(Old English) from Greek *'logike tekhne'* meaning: 'the art of reason.'

Logo–(Old English) from Greek *'logos'* meaning: 'a design or symbol chosen by an organisation to identify its products.'

Lucid–(Old English) from Latin *'lucidus'* meaning: 'bright'

Lucifer–(Old English) Latin meaning 'light–bringing,' from *lux* 'light' and *fer* 'bearing'

Luck–(Old English) from German *'lucke'* meaning: 'good or bad things happen by chance.'

Lunatic–(Old English) from Latin 'luna' meaning: 'moon' (from belief that changes of the moon caused insanity).

Lymph–(Old English) from Latin *'lympha, limpa'* meaning: 'water'

Manicure–(Late 19th Century) adopted from the French word, from Latin *manus* 'hand' and *cura* 'care'

Market–Latin *merx*: meaning 'merchandise'

Monk–(Old English) from late Greek *monachos*, 'a religious hermit,' *monos*, 'alone'

Myriad–(mid 16th Century) originally found as a unit meaning ten thousand. The word came via late Latin from Greek *murias*, muriad, from *murioi* '10,000'

Mystic–(Middle English) from Greek *mustikos*, from *mueo* 'initiated person'

Nefarious–(early 17th century) Latin nefarious, based on *negas*, *nefar*–'wrong' (from *ne*–'not' and *fas* 'divine law')

Nomad–(late 16th Century) Greek *nomas*, 'roaming in search of pasture'

Nostalgia–(late 18th century) 'homesickness,' from Greek *nostos* 'return home' and *algos* 'pain'

Obey–(Middle English) from Latin *oboedire* 'listen, pay attention to'

Ocean–(Middle English) Greek *okeanos* 'great stream encircling the earth's disc'

Occult–(late 15th century) Latin *occultare* 'to hide'

Orb–(late Middle English) from Latin *orbis* 'ring'

Paparazzi–(1960s) this term for freelance photographers who pursue celebrities to obtain lucrative photos of them is from Italian: it comes from the name of a character in *Felini's film La Dolce Vita (1960).*

Pathetic—(late 16th century) Latin from Greek *pathetikos* 'sensitive,' based on *pathos* 'suffering'

Pilgrim—Latin *Pereger:* meaning 'on a journey, travelling though a foreign land,' *per* 'through', and *ager* 'land, country.'

Plague—Greek *plaga*, 'stroke,blow'

Question—(Late Middle English) from Latin *quaerere* 'ask, seek' is the base.

Relax—(Late Middle English) from Latin *relaxare*, based on *laxus* 'lax, loose'

Same—(Middle English) from Sanskrit *sama*

Sandwich—(mid 18th century) derives its name from the *4th Earl of Sandwich (1718–92)*, an English nobleman said to have eaten food in this form so that he would not have to leave the gaming table thereby losing precious time.

Sanity—(late Middle English) Latin *sanus* 'healthy'

Silhouette—(late 18th century) this word comes from the name of *Etienne de Silhouette (1709–67)*, a French author and politician. Silhouette is said to have decorated the walls of his chateau at Bry-sur-Marne.

Sky-(Middle English) Old Norse sky 'cloud'

Superb-(mid 16th century) from Latin *superbus* 'proud, magnificent'

Symmetry-(Old English) from Latin *symmetria* 'the quality of being similar of equal'

Synchronous-(Old English) from Greek *sunkhronos* 'the occurrence of events at the same time'

Synthesis-(early 17th century) from Greek *sunthesis*, from *suntithenai* 'place together'

Talent-(Old English) from Latin *talenta* 'sum of money' (from Greek *talanton*)

Tatoo-(mid 17th century) from Samoan *ta-tau*

Television-(early 20th century) from Greek *tele* 'at a distance,' and the noun vision.

Ugly-(Middle English) Ugly is from the Old Norse *uggligr* 'to be dreaded'

University-Latin *universus*: meaning 'whole'

Vaccine-(late 18th century) from Latin *vaccinus*, from

vacca 'cow,' linked to the early use of the cowpox virus smallpox.

Wicked—(Middle English) from Old English *wicca* 'witch'

Xmas—(mid 18th century) the initial letter X represents the initial letter chi of Greek *Khristos* 'Christ'

Zodiac—(late Middle English) from Greek *zoidiakos*, from *zoidion* 'sculptured animal figure,' zoion 'animal'

Zombie—(early 19th century) from the West African origin: *Kikongo zumbi* 'fetish'

TRYATHON ANIMATION EXCERPTS

I know I've been lied too,

But I was asleep,

An oh yes, the sleep was enjoyable (ha–ha),

But the alarm rang,

I am not frustrated, I'm mad,

But what would anger do on the chessboard?

I'm letting go off everything now,

Free from expectations,

As free as a bird.

The world is on my side, I can feel it,

Our freedom begins tonight,

Everyone sees, but not everyone sees the world with the same lens,

Seeing the world with new eyes, offers—a different vision,

This is the beginning, just the—beginning.

Fear no more,

My eyes are open now,

I must say, the world can seem awfully strange,

When your—lost

No turning back,

I won't go down that road again,

My soul won't—let me.

And this is just the first step—in a billion,

More power, more strength, more—wisdom,

Can you feel me?

Today we dine in abundance, we scream, we roar, and we will be in heaven,

A state of mind: it is not a thing talk—of

Most of what people talk about, can never be verified,

Its only speculation,

So open your mind, and think for yourself,

What's stopping you?

Cast your mind back,

Before time, a world—imagine.

Sometimes, we will face our hardest battles, when we feel our weakest.

Fly—I am ready for anything,

Beyond human—The world sleeps in my palms,

Know Thyself—I'm part of everything.

The deeper you go, the deeper it gets—I know that

much.

"I hear screams from Earth: screams of a billion prisoners: screams of abandoned children from their mothers: What have we become?

We hear everything, Tryathon has seen it all, and we will watch no–further."

They already walk amongst us, the 'Number Makers.'

What's a life worth?

Are there words to describe it?

Have you ever stop to wonder?

I am sure you have heard the story of the fish, striving to understand the nature of water, until it went so far down and realised there was only more–water.

Imagine

A world

Before time

What happens?

When questions flood your mind?

What's your story?

You can–be–anything?

You decide

The world is yours

Keep on flying.

I know not a thing about this world,

To say I do, would be foolish,

However, I do know there are there are worlds beyond this one,

Beyond our vision,

Beyond our comprehension.

Everyone breathes, but not everyone breathes deep enough.

Dreaming realer than reality,

My dreams are realer than—reality.

TRYATHON GALLERY

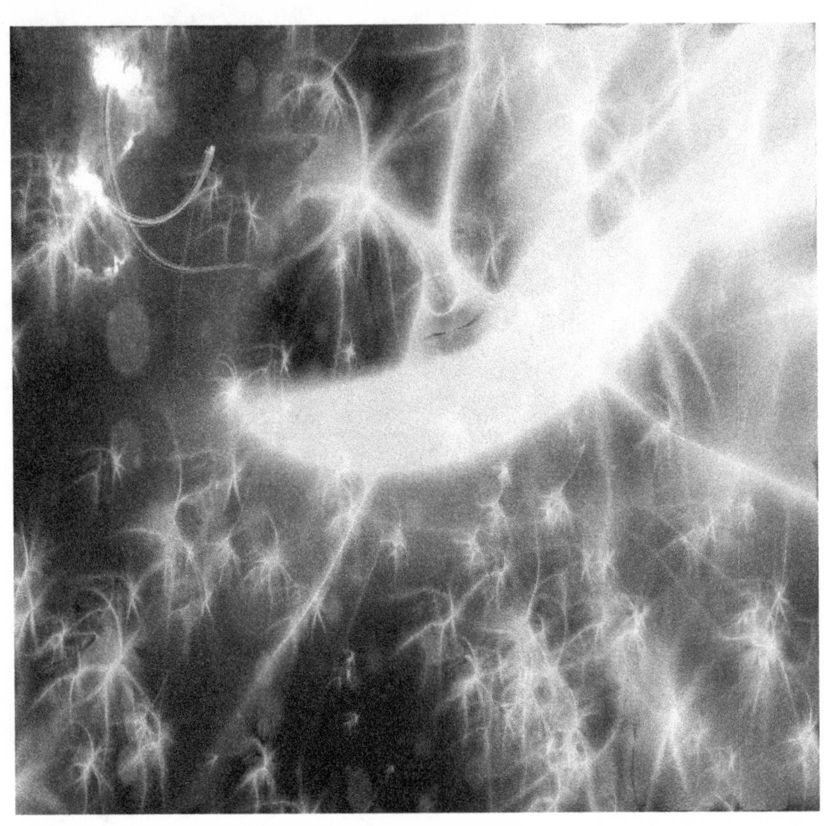

TRYATHON—THE LOVE OF A GALAXY

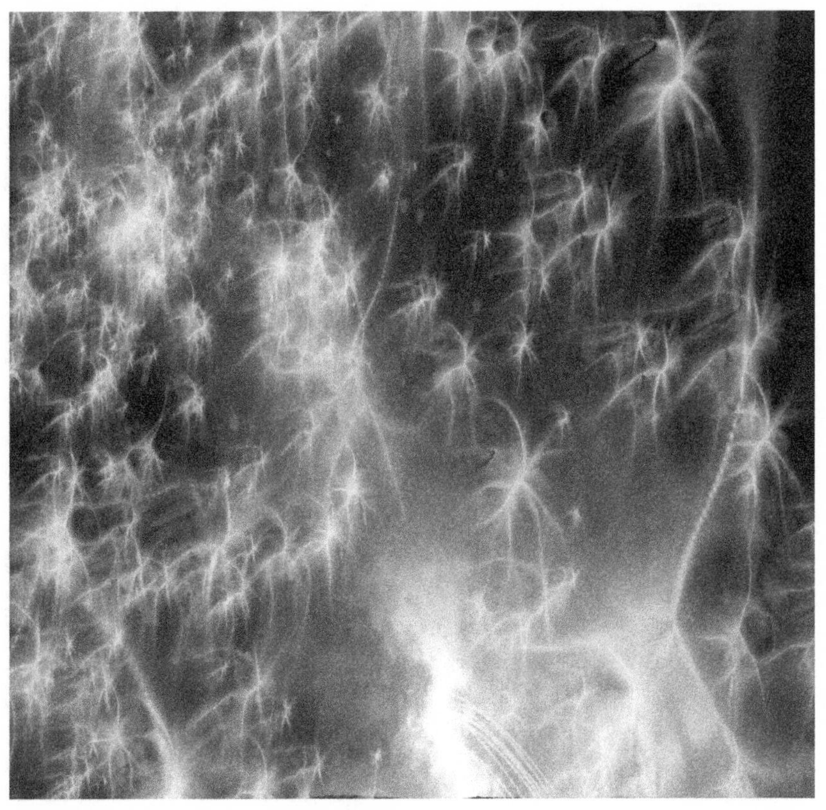

STREAMS OF LIGHT

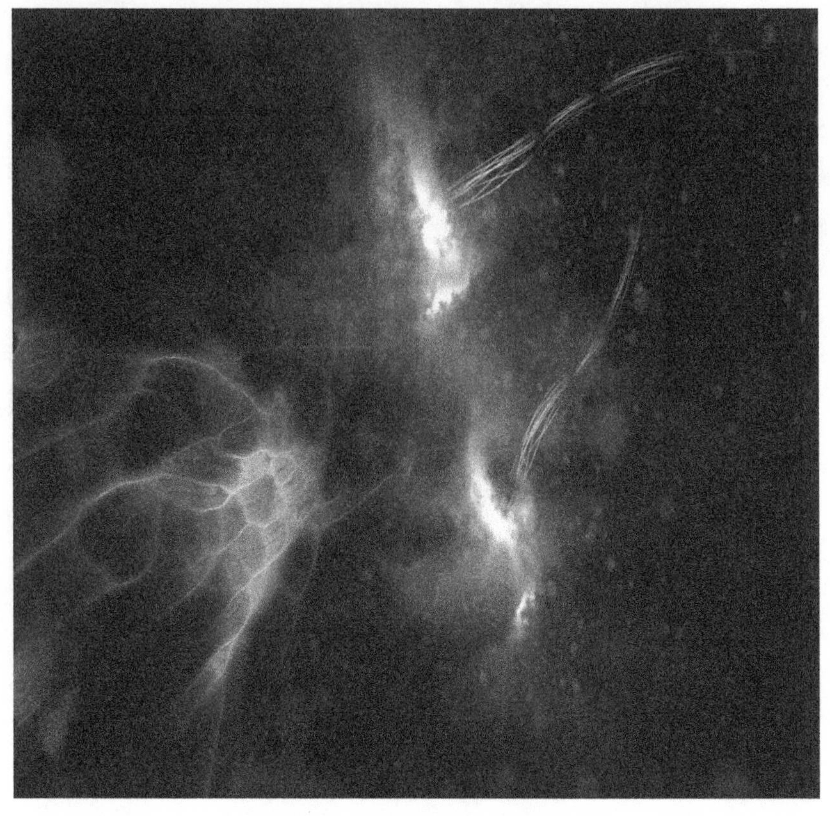

STREAMS OF LIGHT

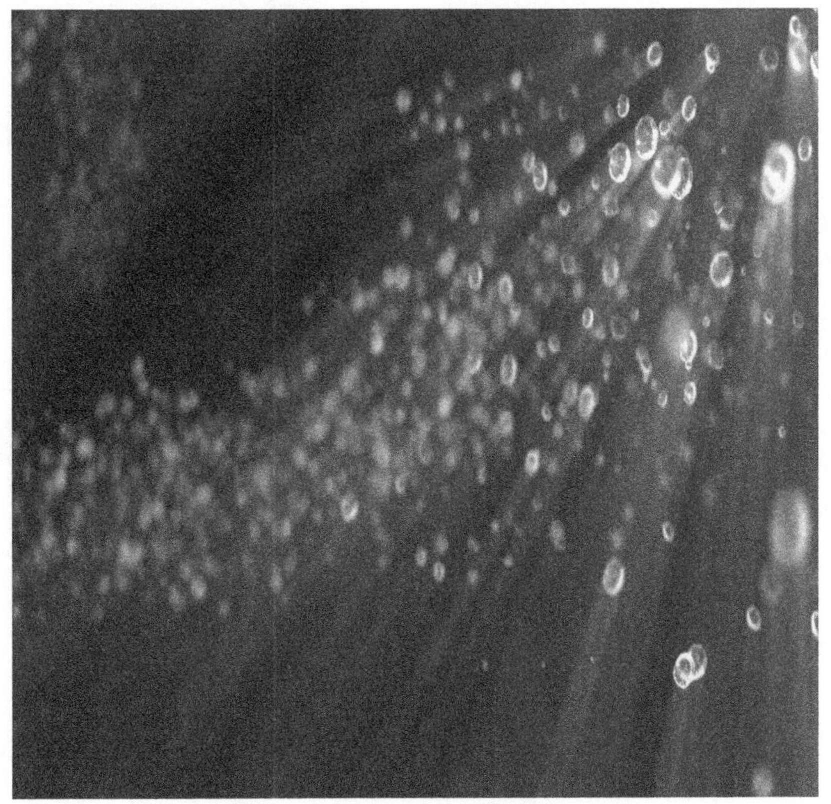

MEMNERS—THE CRYSTALS

MEMNERS—THE CRYSTALS

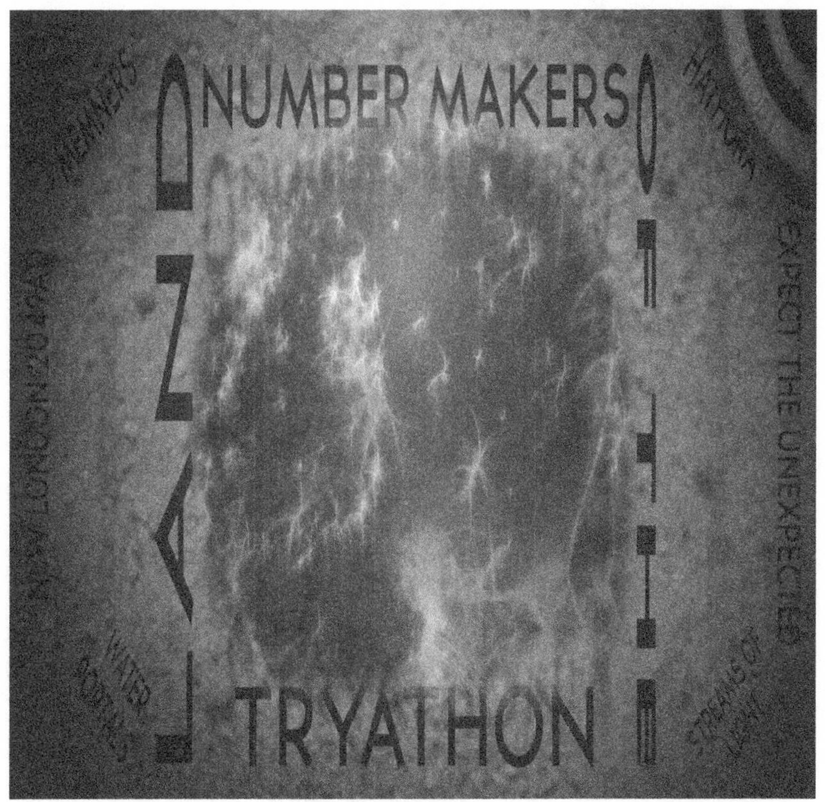

TRYATHON—LAND OF THE NUMBER MAKERS

TRYATHON—LAND OF THE NUMBER MAKERS

NEW LONDON 2049 AD–PATHLESS LAND

NEW LONDON 2049 AD—THE DIGITAL AGE

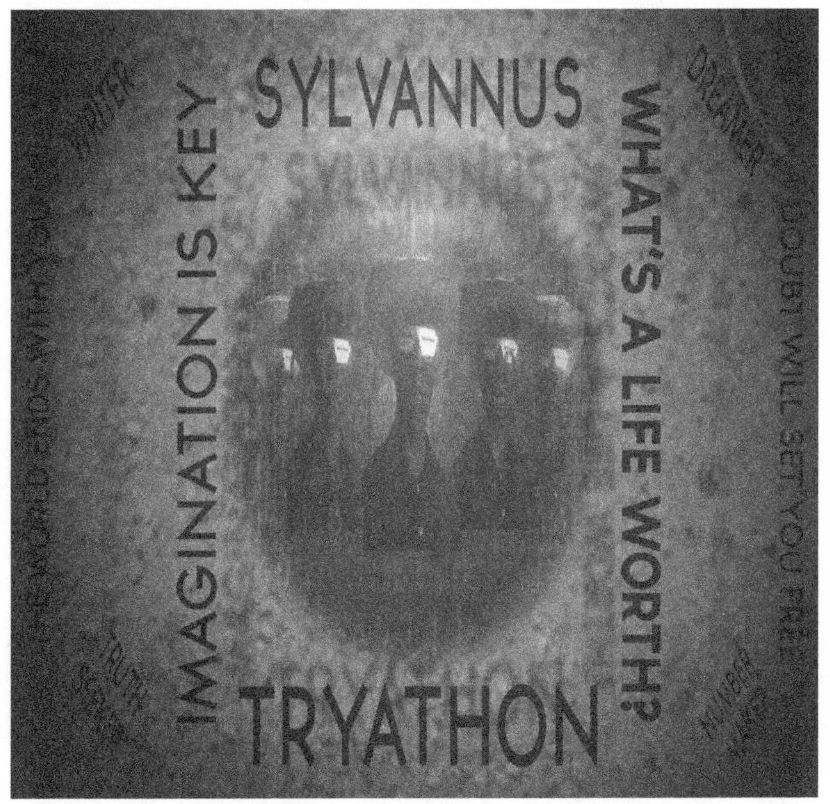

SYLVANNUS–WRITER

PANDORA—WORD ARCHITECT

LUZ–VISIONARY

PROTEUS—HACKER

<u>GOTHLIN–NUMBER MAKER</u>

HATHORA—ORACLE OF TRYATHON

<u>NUMBER MAKERS—ALL WE HAVE IS NOW</u>

SYLVANNUS—EYES WIDE OPEN

LUZ–LETTING GO

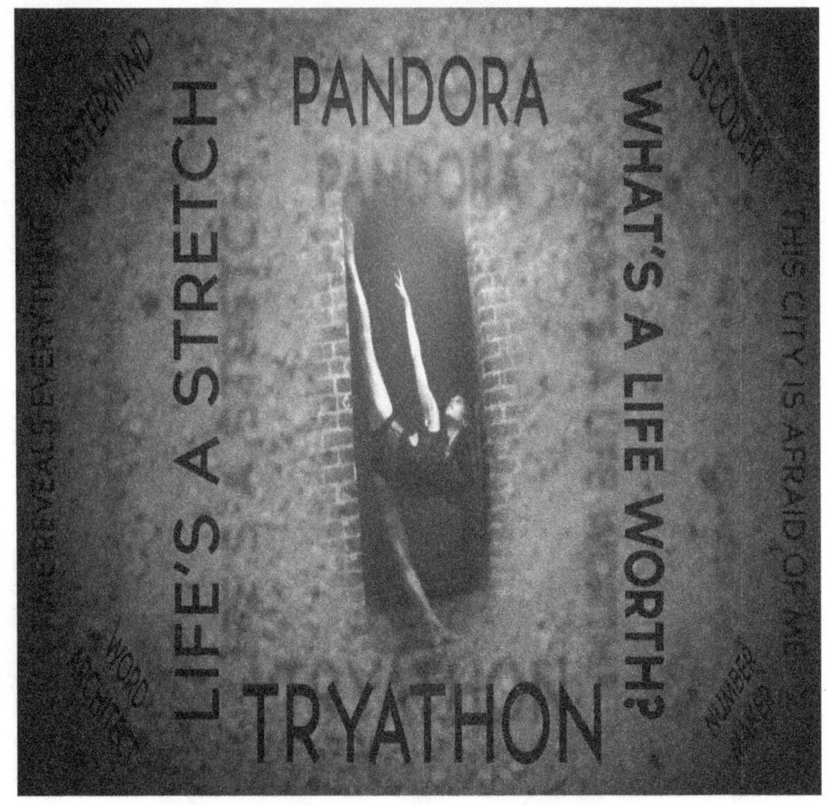

PANDORA—LIFE'S A STRETCH

PRAA SANDS—WATER WORLD

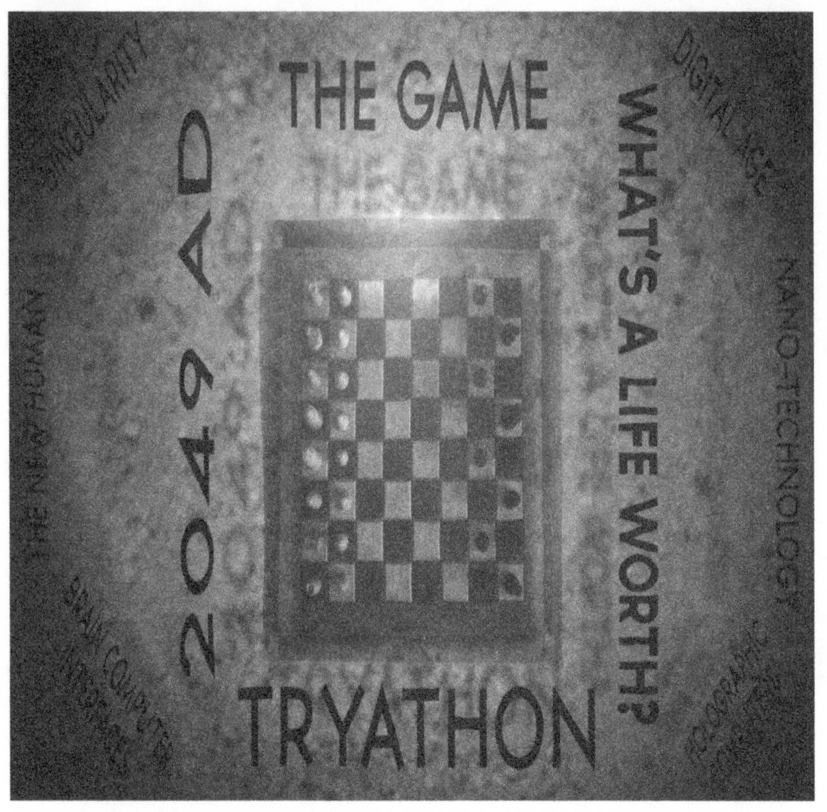

THE GAME OF LIFE—WATCH YOUR MOVE

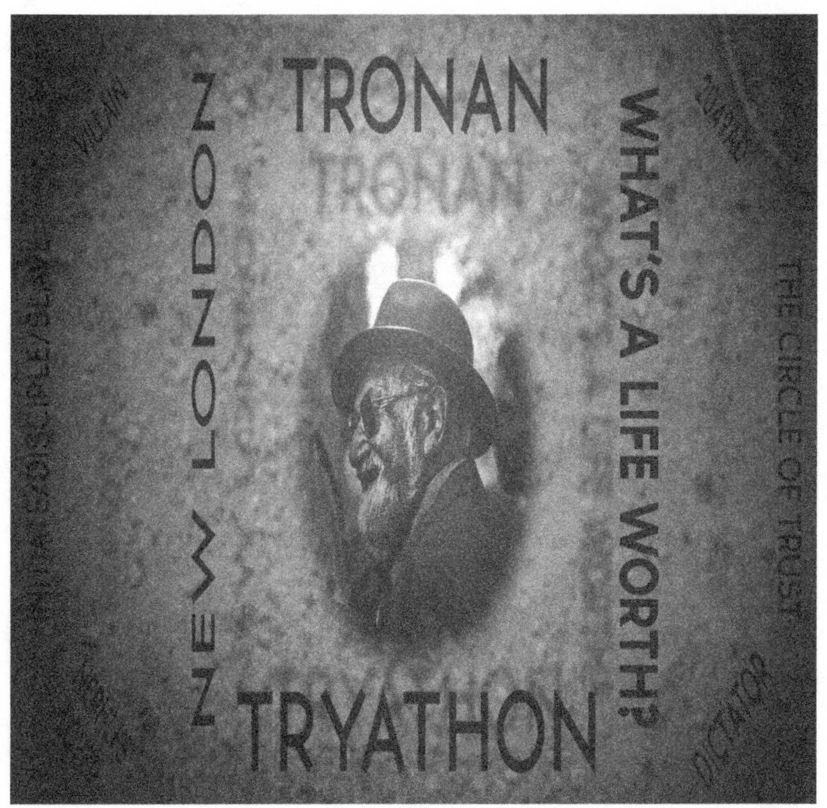

TRONAN—THE CITY IS MINE

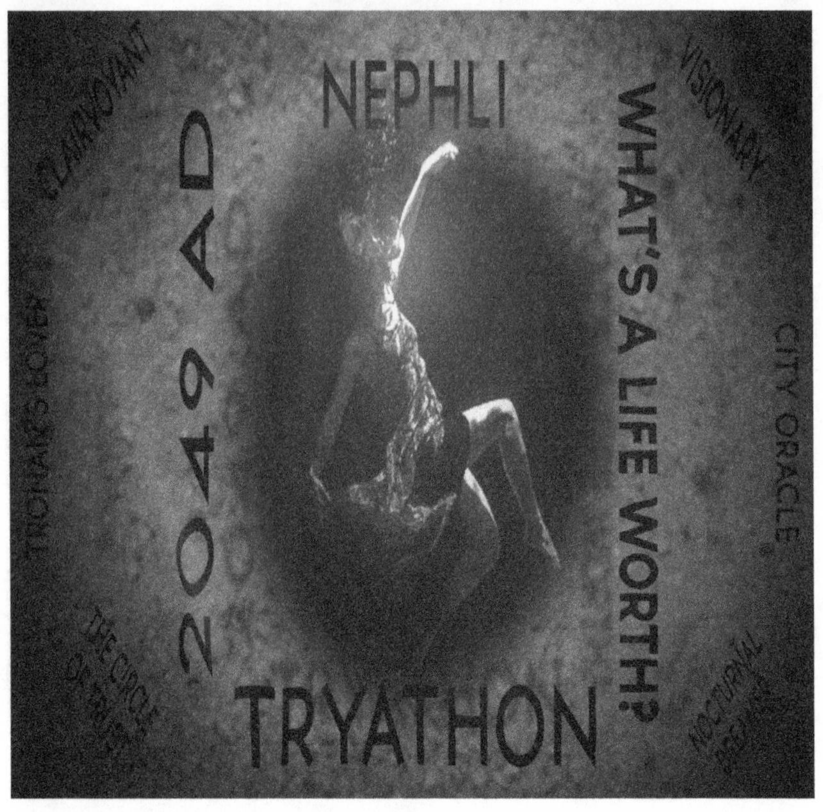

<u>NEPHLI—THE DEEPER YOU GO, THE DEEPER IT GETS</u>

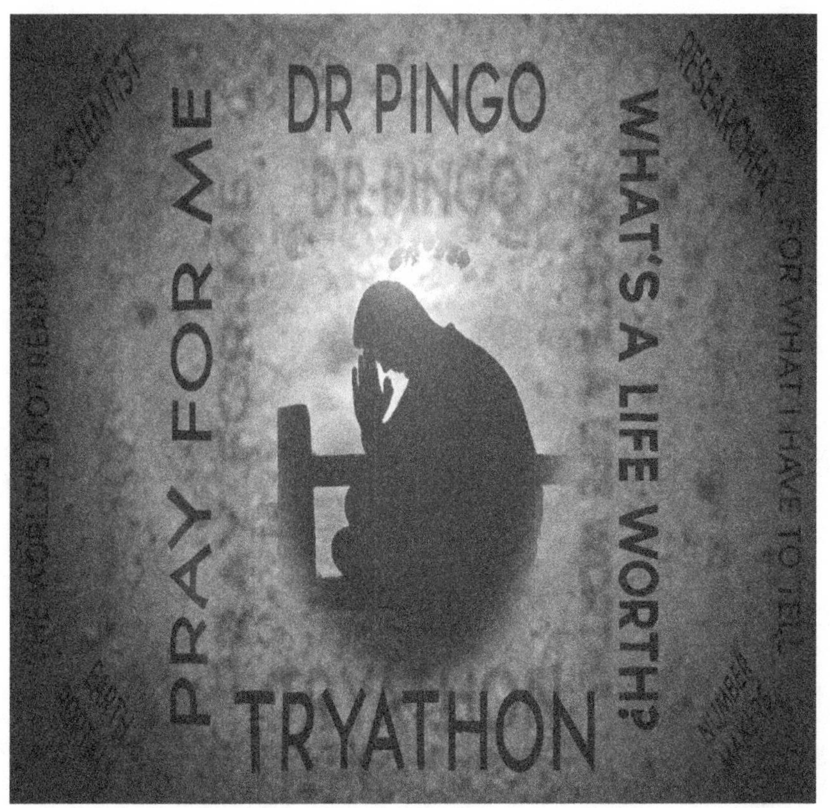

DR. PINGO–PRAY FOR ME

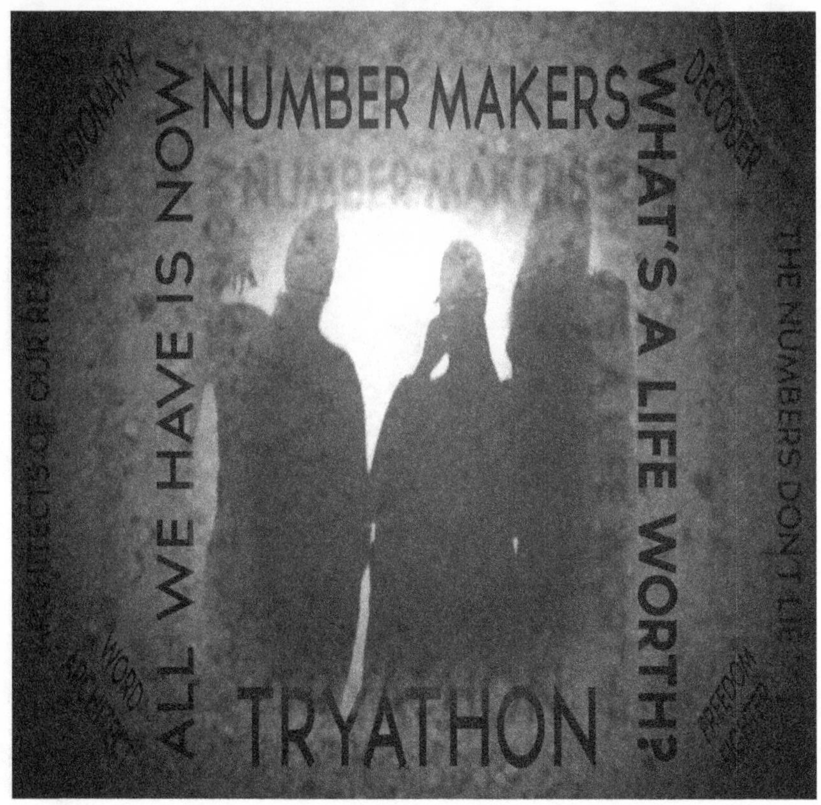

NUMBER MAKERS—ARCHITECTS OF OUR REALITY

THE X-MATRON–MORE THAN JUST A CAR

<u>THE CIRCLE OF TRUST—WE WILL GUIDE YOU</u>

PROTEUS–THERE'S ALWAYS A WAY IN

<u>THE CAVES</u>

TRONAN'S DICE—THE GAME OF LIFE

BLOTIX—MIND TRANSFER

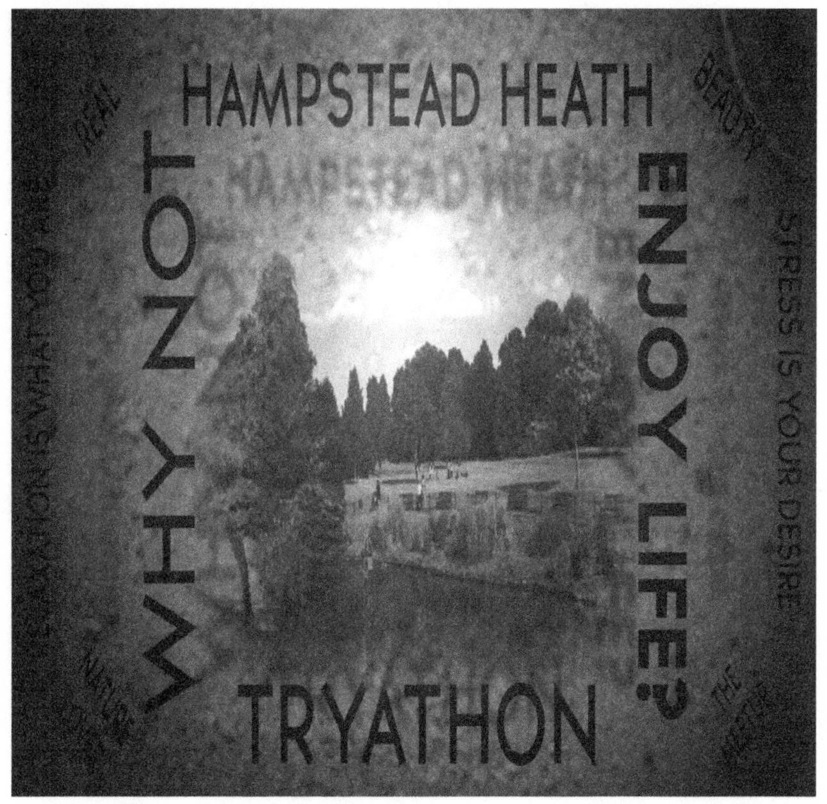

HAMPSTEAD HEATH—WE CAME HERE TO PLAY

SYLVANNUS & LUZ—TOGETHER WE STAND

NUMBER MAKERS–FEARLESS

GOVERNOR OF NEPTIS—SACRIFICE

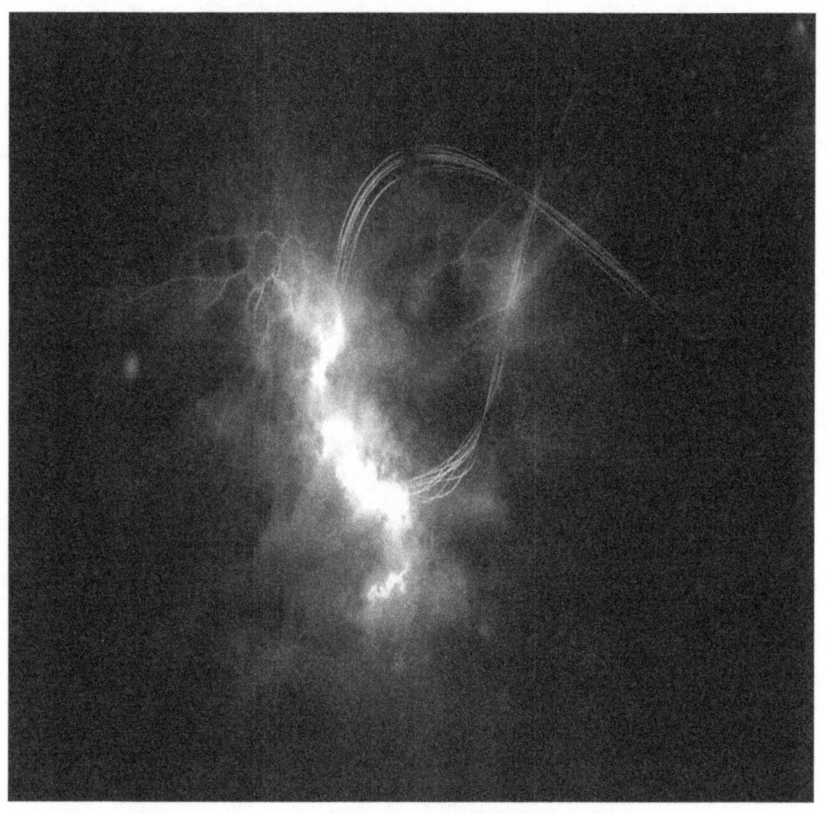

TRYATHON–LIGHT LOVERS

TRYATHON LIGHTS

PRAA SANDS SKYLINE—THE REBIRTH

EXTRA JOURNALS

NOTHING MORE THAN THEATRE

SYLVANNUS'S JOURNAL - JULY 4TH 2049

Nothing more than theatre!

Life is a play, nothing more than theatre; a great stage show.

We write the script and we direct the film.

We are the lead star; we even write the scripts of everyone else in our play.

THE RICH AND THE POOR

SYLVANNUS'S JOURNAL - 2049 AUGUST 12TH

Some of the richest people on this planet are the most generous, because they can afford to be.

I am sure you have heard the expression of the poor miser.

What could the poor possibly give you? What do they have to give?

I never came into this world to suffer.

I came here to be rich beyond measure—a priceless tag.

I live in the realm of the abundance, therefore I will never be poor.

I will never be in lack.

I fear nothing.

What are you afraid of?

Why can you talk to me on the internet, but not in real life?

IT WAS ALL A DREAM

SYLVANNUS'S JOURNAL - 2049 AUGUST 13TH

If life is a dream, what happens when we wake up?

The spirit dies, when the soul ceases to bear fruit.

He is not my problem, she's not my problem, they are not my problem, I am not my problem—there is no problem.

I hate you and I do not know you.

I am told, you are the threat, so I believe: it has become part of my ritual.

We live lifestyles that are over stimulated, drug fuelled: even our food has become poisoned.

Once again, we find ourselves stuck at the crossroads, and the road goes no—further.

Why should I celebrate a holiday when I am told?

Did I blow out birthday candles?

No!

RESISTANCE MAKES STRONGER

SYLVANNUS'S JOURNAL – AUGUST 23RD 2049

I see an ant, but what animates it?

If life is a video game, then who are the controllers?

What does the world not know?

Our possessions become our possessors.

Who offers you freedom, does not really want to be free; freedom is never offered; it is taken.

Is everything we think we are, an illusion?

Our insanity keeps us sane.

A grain of sand contains billions of atoms, which contain billions of atoms.

The planet is a cell, we are the mitochondria.

Architecture is Earth's clothing.

The biggest lawmakers are the biggest lawbreakers.

Man imitated law to govern men, hence government.

The law is there to protect the ones who created it, not those trying to fight it.

Does nature know its nature?

We lay on a bed of roses, only to be pricked by the thorns.

What you fight, you give power to—resistance makes stronger.

To fight something, is to give power over—life force.

How we see the world, is how it response to us.

What do you have except for your judgement?

When they go, you are left with nothing—a hollow void.

THE SEARCH

SYLVANNUS'S JOURNAL - AUGUST 31ST 2049

The problem with the search, is you always have to go outside of yourself.

This is a spiritual war we face—a battle for hearts and minds.

Who has our minds? Who controls them?

I'm not a scholar—however, from time to time I ponder the question of truth.

I tend to think the truth is the period between—sleeping and waking, the in between.

Half of our lives our spent dreaming about what we want to achieve; the other half is spent worrying about if we will ever get it.

I live like I already have.

You can only lose, what does not belong to you.

There is nothing to see, but what you put there.

A man will only catch a woman, when she catches him.

The body is a projection of the mind.

Physical death is an illusion.

The only death, is the death of images, all that the ego has formed to maintain its own continuity.

IMAGINATION IS KEY

SYLVANNUS'S JOURNAL - SEPTEMBER 1ST 2049

Intellect is known, imagination is infinite.

The only conspiracy against you, is the one you already know, because you created it.

The mask is the image we have of ourselves.

Is there any way to listen to anything without interpretation?

Are we working ourselves towards our own extinction?

Parents really don't have a clue, when they feel their child's irrational behaviour, results from them not finding a suitable job.

We are all programmed.

The only way to be free of the programming, is to know one is programmed, and begin deprogramming.

The human body is made up of trillions of cells, however, one cell can store us much information as the most powerful computer on Earth, and still have space to move around.

How do you think a child is born?

NO WISE MEN—NO WISE WOMEN

SYLVANNUS'S JOURNAL - SEPTEMBER 2ND 2049

There are no wise men, no wise women—only those who have created enough silence to hear the truth.

Only without opposition, can one wander freely along the chessboard: we are governed by everything around us.

When a mind sees its own pettiness, then it begins to grow.

I live as if I have achieved nothing, and I will die as if I have achieved—everything.

SAILING BEYOND KNOWLEDGE

SYLVANNUS'S JOURNAL - SEPTEMBER 3RD 2049

The world is perception based: you need an opinion to maintain the continuity of your imaginary existence.

Your opinion creates an image of yourself in your head.

A child has no opinion—no world.

You think, because you do not know.

I would love to have a conversation with every single person on this planet.

Maybe they might tell me all the same, or maybe they might have some different to tell—I wonder.

THE CHILD SACRIFICE

SYLVANNUS'S JOURNAL – SEPTEMBER 4TH 2049

Great artists do not use energy to create works, but create energy from their works.

You attract whatever you fear to you, just as whatever you love.

Thoughts are attractions, tangible realities.

But when you are not thinking, what are you attracting, or do we become our own attractions?

Humanity's nightmare!

Why are we birthing chaos on the planet?

Why do we sacrifice our children and send them to the slaughter house?

THE GRAND DECEPTION

SYLVANNUS'S JOURNAL – SEPTEMBER 5TH 2049

If wearing clothes was our first deception, what was the second?

Can we unlearn our naked shame?

A lie can only be told, if you know the truth.

We are all equal in death.

This city has turned me into a monster.

I feel compelled to set my legacy in stone.

In the city, I only see concrete; I only see rigid attitudes.

We cover the ground with concrete, so divine water cannot touch soil.

Are we nature's food?

Were we set up to fail?

I am losing sight of myself in this—digital world.

The end of the world is nigh.

The world is the idea: all ideas must—change.

NOTE FROM THE AUTHOR

Ralph Smart was born in London. He has travelled to every continent except Asia. He enjoys nature and meeting people from all spectrums of life. Awarded with a 'BA Combined Honours' in 'Psychology' and 'Criminology'—human nature fascinates him. Tryathon is the first novel in the Tryathon series. He would love to connect with readers interested in knowing more about Tryathon: he can be contacted at: www.infinitewaters@gmail.com. Also a motion graphics artist and filmmaker: Tryathon animations can be found on his 'you tube page,' as well as other upcoming film projects: www.youtube.com/kemetprince1. The official 'Tryathon' website can be found at: www.tryathon.com. Feel free to join the online forum, which would be a great place to meet new people, and discuss the latest information regarding 'future emerging technology.' Life is to be—enjoyed.

STAY DIVING INTO INFINITE WATERS

CPSIA information can be obtained
at www.ICGtesting.com
Printed in the USA
LVHW090225120420
653129LV00001B/23